"What in the hell are you doing?" Charlotte screamed, tightening her grip on the wheel.

The other vehicle darted over into the left lane, despite it being a two-way street. Its engine roared as the car picked up speed.

They rode side by side. She slowed, and it slowed, so she pressed down on the accelerator while struggling not to run off the road. Charlotte reached for her phone to call Miles. But it was inside her purse, which had flown into the back seat.

The car crept closer to Charlotte's. She skidded over the edge of the desert. A blanket of gravel enveloped her sedan. She veered back and forth, the steering wheel taking on a life of its own. The passenger side of her car rode the shoulder. The attacker's vehicle was inches away from the driver's side. He had her hemmed in. A collision was looming, unless she drove farther into the pitch-black desert...

DANGER IN THE NEVADA DESERT

———

DENISE N. WHEATLEY

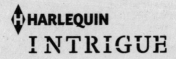

This book is dedicated to my fifth-grade teacher,
Mrs. Myra Blouin, who convinced me that I could
accomplish anything.

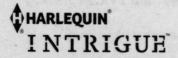

ISBN-13: 978-1-335-58269-0

Danger in the Nevada Desert

Copyright © 2023 by Denise N. Wheatley

Recycling programs
for this product may
not exist in your area.

For questions and comments about the quality of this book,
please contact us at CustomerService@Harlequin.com.

Harlequin Enterprises ULC
22 Adelaide St. West, 41st Floor
Toronto, Ontario M5H 4E3, Canada
www.Harlequin.com

Printed in U.S.A.

Denise N. Wheatley loves happy endings and the art of storytelling. Her novels run the romance gamut, and she strives to pen entertaining books that embody matters of the heart. She's an RWA member and holds a BA in English from the University of Illinois. When Denise isn't writing, she enjoys watching true-crime TV and chatting with readers. Follow her on social media.

Instagram: @Denise_Wheatley_Writer
Twitter: @DeniseWheatley
BookBub: @DeniseNWheatley
Goodreads: Denise N. Wheatley

Books by Denise N. Wheatley

Harlequin Intrigue

A West Coast Crime Story

The Heart-Shaped Murders
Danger in the Nevada Desert

Cold Case True Crime
Bayou Christmas Disappearance
Backcountry Cover-Up

Visit the Author Profile page at Harlequin.com.

CAST OF CHARACTERS

Miles Love—A Clemmington, California, police detective.

Charlotte Bowman—A police sergeant in River Valley, Nevada, who's on the hunt for a serial killer.

Walter Kincaid—A River Valley corporal and Charlotte's ex-boyfriend.

Ethan Mitchell—River Valley's chief of police.

Ella Bowman—Charlotte's sister, who works as a traveling nurse.

Stephen Seymour—The Nevada district attorney's son.

Jake Love—A Clemmington detective and Miles's brother.

Lena Love—A Clemmington forensic investigator and Miles's sister.

Kennedy Love—Clemmington's chief of police and Miles's father.

If you want to know what a killer looks like, go look in the mirror.

—Lieutenant Tony Mullins, Memphis Police
Department

Prologue

Police Sergeant Charlotte Bowman climbed down the trail of Glacier Lake's campsite, careful not to roll her ankle on the rugged terrain like she had the last time.

The sun was setting on the beautiful grounds, nestled in between the majestic River Mountains. Beams of light glistened off the shimmering blue water, illuminating the canyon's colorful wildflowers and crystalline gemstones.

The lake's surroundings made for the perfect afternoon getaway. Charlotte wished she were there for one. But instead, she was investigating the latest murder committed by the Numeric Serial Killer.

Tendrils of jet-black curls stuck to her perspiring neck. Charlotte swiped them up toward her bun and fanned her face. The one-hundred-degree temperatures of River Valley, Nevada were unrelenting. She'd dressed for the police station's air-conditioned office, not an impromptu trip to the scorching crime scene.

While pulling off her denim jacket and tying it around her waist, Charlotte lost her footing. She skidded along the jagged gray dirt, the thick soles on her hiking boots kicking up clouds of dust. A nearby boulder saved her from falling to the ground.

Charlotte steadied herself, then proceeded down the path. A surge of adrenaline coursed through her body when a desert willow appeared up ahead. Its twisted, forty-foot-tall trunk opened into an elaborate canopy of stunning dark pink blooms. Long, slender twigs fluttered in the breeze, blowing fragrant waves of violet through the air.

The tree's beauty was overshadowed, however, by the memory of Brad Ellington's lifeless body lying underneath its branches. The circumstances surrounding his death were peculiar. There was no trauma to the body. He was fully clothed, without a speck of dirt on his pristine gray Polo shirt, khaki pants and white sneakers. His wallet, keys and identification were still in his pockets, making him easily identifiable.

And proving this was no robbery. So, what was it about?

The biggest oddity was the number nine that had been carved into his left cheek. Its edges were jagged, as if cut with a dull object. Charlotte had seen a lot during her fourteen years in law enforcement, but there was something about the barbaric scar that chilled her to the core.

You're doing it again. No emotions, remember? Stick to the business at hand.

Charlotte pulled on a pair of latex gloves and approached the tree. River Valley's chief of police, Ethan Mitchell, had sent her back out to the scene to try and collect more DNA. She'd tried to tell him that the team had combed the area numerous times. The only evidence worth gathering was a few clumps of blood-soaked dirt. The results came back identifying only one profile, and that was Brad's.

"There's got to be something more out there," Chief Mitchell had insisted, his bushy silver eyebrows shooting up toward his receding hairline.

Charlotte knew that look. It meant an order had been given and the conversation was over.

And now here I am, trying to pull off a magic trick and make evidence appear that just isn't here...

A dark cloud drifted in front of the setting sun, blocking its fading light. Charlotte grabbed a flashlight from her black cargo pants and turned on her body cam.

"This is Sergeant Bowman, reporting from the Glacier Lake campgrounds where Brad Ellington's body was found. Per Chief Mitchell's request, I am searching the scene for additional evidence—"

Loud footsteps thumped behind her. Charlotte stopped abruptly and pivoted. No one was there.

Am I hearing things?

The campsite had cleared out now that dusk was settling. Fishermen's boats were docked, jet skis stored and charcoal grills extinguished. There were no visitors in sight.

Charlotte turned her attention back to the hollow at the base of the tree trunk. *Just see what you can find and get the hell out of here...*

"I am standing near the desert willow where the deceased victim was recovered, attempting to collect anything that will link our suspect to the scene. I'll be scanning the soil and gathering additional samples for blood evidence, bodily fluids, footprints, hair, fibers..."

Everything that we've already searched for, she resisted the urge to add.

Charlotte bent down and scooped up a clump of earth. She shined her light on the specimen. Nothing jumped out at her. She packed it inside of a plastic bag anyway.

Creak!

The sound of crackling bark screeched overhead. Charlotte leapt to her feet, hoping to avoid a falling branch. The air grew still. And silent, except for the leaves swishing in the wind. Nevertheless, Charlotte spun a one-eighty in search of a lurker. No one was there.

You're being paranoid...

She bent down and scooped another sample of soil.

Bam!

"Dammit!" Charlotte yelled, gripping the back of her head.

She tumbled onto her knees. Her eyes darted in search of the branch that had knocked her to the ground. Charlotte attempted to roll over and pull herself back up. But she was stopped by a pair of hands.

An excruciating squeeze to her shoulders pushed her into the dirt. Charlotte released a piercing scream but was quickly silenced when a hand covered her mouth.

A heavy body pounced on top of her. Pressed her face into the ground.

"Stop!" Charlotte attempted to yell before being muffled by the soil.

"You're coming with me," a deep, trembling voice sputtered in her ear.

"The hell I am!" she barked.

The assailant grabbed a chunk of her hair, pulling her face out of the dirt.

"What did you just say to me?" he growled.

She choked, spitting a mouthful of soil onto the ground. "I said I'm not going with—"

He shoved her face into the dirt. Charlotte reached back, struggling to jab him with her elbow. He didn't budge.

Her passageways constricted as she gasped for air. Particles of dirt invaded the sparse streams of oxygen trickling down her throat. Charlotte felt herself fading to black. Just when she thought she might pass out, the man grabbed her arm, forcing her to stand.

"Go," he spat. *"Move!"*

He shoved her up the terrain toward the parking lot. Charlotte's slim wrists were bound behind her back, held together within his tight grip.

You have got to get away from this man. He is going to kill you. Fight!

Her head swiveled when a family climbed inside a nearby car. The attacker's grasp tightened.

"Don't even *think* about calling for help. Try it and I'll snap your neck right here on the spot."

The sobering threat dampened Charlotte's will to fight. A scream crept up her throat, but she suppressed it. She had no doubt this man would not only kill her but that innocent family, too, if she resisted. She swallowed, craning her neck to get a better look at the assailant. His baggy black clothing and dirt bike mask made it nearly impossible. The only two things Charlotte could make out were his tall frame and dark, dead eyes.

"You won't get away with this," she uttered. "Do you realize who I am?"

He emitted a sinister chuckle. "Of course I do. You're Sergeant Charlotte Bowman."

A burst of fear detonated inside her chest. Charlotte's knees buckled underneath the weight of him speaking her name. She almost fell to the ground before he yanked her back up.

"*Walk!* Don't make this harder than it has to be."

Tears of anger burned Charlotte's eyes. She knew better. Her guard should've been up. But stress and fatigue had gotten the best of her. Charlotte had naively shown up at the crime scene alone, thinking the visit would be just as uneventful as all the others, despite the numerous threats she'd been receiving.

The harassment had begun the moment she was promoted to sergeant and revved up once she took over the serial killer case. Suspicions of her fellow law enforcement officers swirled in the back of her mind. But now Charlotte realized she could've been wrong. Maybe it had been the suspect she was after threatening her all along.

Just as the assailant dragged her toward the middle of the parking lot, a little girl hopped out of a car.

"Mommy! I left my bucket down by the water!"

"Isabella!" a woman yelled, running after her. "Come back here!"

"Get down!" Charlotte's attacker hissed, forcing her to duck behind a pickup truck. Before Charlotte could bend over, the woman turned in their direction.

"Ma'am?" she called out. "Are you okay?"

"Shut your mouth!" the suspect insisted.

A man climbed out of the car. His eyes darted back and forth between Charlotte and her assailant. "What's going on here? Miss, do you need some help?"

The assailant pushed Charlotte to the ground and ran off. The couple charged toward her.

"Kurt," the woman yelled. "Call 9-1-1!" She helped Charlotte to her feet. "We'll stay with you until the authorities get here."

"Thank you," Charlotte panted, too overwhelmed to tell the woman that she herself was law enforcement.

Chapter One

Miles slammed his laptop shut and glanced down at his watch. It was almost seven o'clock. He grabbed his cell phone and texted his mother, letting her know he'd be late for their family dinner.

Just as he hit the send button, the phone rang. The call was coming from a Nevada area code. He didn't recognize the number but picked up anyway.

"Hello?"

"Hi. Um—Officer Love?"

The woman's soft voice sounded somewhat familiar. "It's Detective Love, actually. I was recently promoted. May I ask who I'm speaking to?"

"Oh. Congratulations on the promotion. This is Charlotte. Charlotte Bowman."

The phone almost slipped from his hand.

"Char-*Charlotte*? Hey…hi—hello," he stammered, his chest tightening. "What a surprise. How are you?"

"I'm okay. I could be better. Which is why I'm calling you."

Miles paused, his skin prickling with curiosity as he thought back on the moment they'd met.

The pair crossed paths a few years ago at the Southwestern Law Enforcement Education and Technology Conference. Charlotte was attending on behalf of River Valley PD. They were partnered up during a combative suspect training session, and the energy between them was magnetic. Miles could still remember the shivers of excitement that shot through his body when Charlotte spun him around, patted him down and placed him in handcuffs.

That partnership led to dinner later that evening, which led to a nightcap in her hotel room and, ultimately, the pair making love. Afterward, Miles found out that Charlotte was recently divorced. She wasn't ready for a relationship. Once the conference ended, so did their brief yet passionate tryst.

Upon returning to Clemmington, Miles found himself pining after Charlotte. He couldn't get her off his mind. But he'd resisted the urge to contact her and they never spoke again. Until now.

"I'm shocked to hear from you," he said.

"I know. A lot of time has passed. And a lot has changed in my life since we met."

She hesitated. Miles held his breath, eager to hear where this conversation was going.

"Plus," she continued after several beats, "I need you."

He shot straight up in his chair. "You need me? Why? What's going on?"

"I don't know if you've heard, but we've got a serial killer on the loose in Nevada. His last two murders occurred right here in River Valley."

"Oh, wow. No, I hadn't heard. We'd been busy here

working to catch that California serial killer who attacked my sister, Lena."

"Yeah, I read about that. I'm so sorry, Miles. But good on Lena for putting up an amazing fight. And congratulations to your entire family on the arrest. You were a pretty integral part of that takedown, weren't you?"

"Thank you. And yes, I was."

Miles stood up and walked over to the window. Fall was approaching, and the black oak tree leaves were already turning a deep reddish orange. The park district's decorating committee had propped their giant scarecrow near the wrought iron entryway gates. Faux jumbo pumpkins and square bales of hay had been scattered throughout the lawn.

His gaze drifted toward a family heading to the playground, lovingly holding hands. A deep longing twitched inside his chest. He quickly turned away. "So, you mentioned something about needing me?"

"Yes. I did. I was recently promoted to sergeant, and—"

"Wait, you were? To *sergeant*? That is huge, Charlotte. Congratulations are in order to you, too."

"Thank you. But you know how the saying goes. 'To whom much is given, much is expected.' Shortly after I was promoted, this serial killer case landed on my desk. And honestly, I feel like I'm in over my head. Since you just went through a similar investigation, I was hoping you could lend me your expertise. Maybe develop a partnership of sorts."

A flurry of emotions hit, sending Miles back down into his chair. Partnering up with Charlotte would mean reconnecting, talking on a regular basis, possibly meeting in person...

"I was hoping you'd consider flying out to River Valley and spending some time here in town," Charlotte continued. "If you can, of course. You're probably swamped after being promoted—"

"I'm not, actually," Miles interjected faster than he'd intended. "I mean, things have slowed down quite a bit since the big arrest. Now that summer's come to an end, it's pretty dead around the station. So..."

"*So*, does that mean you'd be willing to come on board with me and help catch this killer? I've already gotten the approval from my chief."

Miles paused. Charlotte could have consulted with an expert whose primary focus was serial killers. Yet she'd chosen him.

A wave of exhilaration swelled in his chest.

Could this be about more than just business?

"Of course I'll come on board with you," he blurted out before squeezing his eyes shut.

Slow down. She already hurt you once. Don't leave yourself open for it to happen again.

Instead of lamenting over his zealous reaction, Miles scooted closer to the desk and pulled out a notebook. "Tell me about the suspect. What do you know about him so far?"

"He's very similar to the serial killer you just arrested. Organized, premeditated and mission oriented. But the difference is he's murdering young women *and* men. The victims are athletic, professional, and seem to go missing during nights out on the town. But a number of days will go by between the time they disappear and the time they're found."

"What's the main cause of death? Shooting? Stabbing? Strangulation?"

"That's what we're trying to figure out. There's been no trauma to the bodies. So we're thinking that they've been poisoned with an undetectable substance. But here's where things get strange. All of the victims have been found near bodies of water. And there's a number carved into one of their cheeks. In every case, that figure has equaled the number of days between the victim going missing and their date of death."

"Damn," Miles uttered, frantically taking notes. "This guy sounds pretty twisted."

"He is. And much like your killer, there is virtually no evidence left at the crime scenes. That's been our biggest challenge." Charlotte inhaled sharply. "So, what do you think? Are you up for this?"

"Yes. I am absolutely up for this."

"Thank God," Charlotte breathed. "How soon can you get here?"

The excitement in her voice ignited a tingling that coursed through Miles's entire body.

Take it easy. Deep breath...

"First, I have to talk to my chief and the rest of the department," he said. "Make sure my absence won't be a problem."

"Is your father still the chief?"

"He is. I'm surprised you remember that."

"I remember a lot..."

Miles didn't respond immediately. Instead, he sat in silence, relishing the flirtation in her tone.

"Are you still there?" Charlotte asked.

"I'm here. Sorry. I, uh—I'm actually heading to my parents' house now for dinner. I'll run all this by my dad while I'm there and see what he says. If he's down with it, then we'll take it from there."

"And by *take it from there*, I'm hoping you mean you'll hop on a flight and meet me here in River Valley first thing in the morning."

"I don't know about all that," Miles rebutted, chuckling at her enthusiasm. "Let's start with me locking in your number and calling you as soon as I know more."

"That sounds good. I'm looking forward to hearing back from you. And hopefully working with you, Detective Love."

"Same here, Sergeant Bowman. Talk soon."

Miles disconnected the call and stared up at the ceiling, his breathing quickening at the thought of reconnecting with Charlotte.

Bring it down. Remember, it's just business…

Chapter Two

"How's the case coming along, angel?"

Charlotte looked up from her desk. Corporal Walter Kincaid, her colleague and ex-boyfriend, was hovering in her office doorway. His rumpled expression reeked of faux concern.

"Don't you mean Sergeant Bowman?" she snapped. "We talked about this, Corporal. Please show me some respect."

"My apologies, *Sergeant Bowman*. I guess I haven't shaken that adorable little pet name I gave you back when we were dating. Permission to enter?"

Charlotte cringed at the sarcastic tone in his voice. Walter's resentment toward her had been unrelenting ever since she'd been promoted.

"Sure. Come in."

She slammed her laptop shut, not wanting him to see that she'd been reading the latest article published by the *River Valley Voice* on the Numeric Serial Killer. It was scathing, just like all the others.

River Valley's most prolific serial killer in history strikes again as he continues to elude the town's bumbling police department.

Reading that felt like a swift uppercut. Charlotte and her team had been working overtime trying to capture the killer. Nevertheless, they were failing. And the media refused to let them forget it.

Miles, please get here. Fast!

"*Hello*, earth to Charlotte," Walter said, waving his hands before plopping down into a chair. "You still with me? Looks like you drifted off into space or something."

She glared at him, wondering what she'd ever seen in the smug wise guy. Walter had been with the force for almost two years before Charlotte joined. The moment she laid eyes on the Taye Diggs doppelgänger, there was an immediate attraction. But she'd fought it. In the beginning, at least.

Charlotte had promised herself that she'd never date a coworker. But Walter's constant flirting and dry sense of humor eventually wore her down. After months of turning him away, she'd finally agreed to coffee. That mocha latte at Drip & Sip led to weekly lunches, which led to dinners and drinks, and eventually, a relationship.

But after a year of petty arguments over whose turn it was to do the dishes, to more intense jealousy and control issues, Charlotte realized that she'd made a mistake. She cut things off with Walter and never looked back.

He, however, insisted that he could change and begged for a second chance. When that didn't work, he tried partnering with her on the Numeric Serial Killer case. Charlotte turned down his offer. Walter had been on her ever since, offering up unsolicited advice on how to handle the investigation in an attempt to worm his way back into her life.

"What can I do for you, Corporal Kincaid?" she asked, flipping open a file and focusing on it rather than him.

"Why so formal? Let's not act like you and I weren't sharing the same bed almost every day of the week, and—"

"Walter!"

"Ahh, that's more like it. I love hearing you call me by my first name."

"Keep it up and I'll be filing a complaint against you with Chief Mitchell. Now, once again, why are you in my office?"

"*Damn* you're a hard nut to crack," Walter muttered under his breath while scrolling through his cell phone. "Speaking of which, I know you're having a tough time trying to crack this case, and the media's been eating you alive with all the negative reporting."

He's trying to get a rise out of you. Don't let him…

"Where are you going with this?" she asked.

"Just let me finish. I know you don't want my help with this case—"

"Hold on. That is not true. Help is one thing. But you asked if we could partner up on the investigation. That's a completely different scenario. Now, please continue."

The right side of Walter's neck began to pulsate. Charlotte remembered how that would happen every time he became agitated.

"I've been doing some research on the Smiley Face Killer," he said. "Have you heard of him?"

"Of course I have. And I don't think it's just a *him*. I believe those murders are being committed by a group of people who're scattered all over the United States. They've been at it since 1997."

Walter rolled his eyes. "Here you go with one of your deep dive rants…" He slid his cell across the desk. A Wikipedia article titled *"Smiley Face Murder Theory"* appeared on the screen. "Look, my point is, the Smiley Face Killer could be committing these murders here in Nevada. Think about it. All of our victims have been found near bodies of water. They all went missing days before the dates of their deaths. The cause of their deaths has been undetermined. All of that sounds like the work of the Smiley Face Killer to me."

"Thanks for the input," Charlotte said, pushing the phone back across the desk, "but I do not think this is the work of the Smiley Face Killers. First off, they only murder young men. Our suspect is murdering men and women. Secondly, their victims are usually found floating in water with smiley faces drawn somewhere nearby. Our victims have been placed on the shores with numbers carved into their cheeks, and not a smiley face in sight. Third—"

"*Okay*, okay," Walter grunted, snatching up his cell. "I get it. You think I'm wrong. What else is new? Anything to keep me from working this case with you."

The shrill ringing of her phone interrupted the conversation.

"I'll let you take that," he muttered before jumping up and heading toward the door.

It was another trait of his that Charlotte had gotten used to—him running off whenever he felt wronged or embarrassed.

She picked up her cell and answered without checking the caller ID.

"Sergeant Bowman speaking."

"Hello, Charlotte. It's Miles."

She jolted forward and gripped the arm of her chair. "Hey! Please tell me you're at the airport and on the way here."

"Umm, I'm fine. Thanks for asking. How are you?" he asked, chuckling softly.

That quiet laughter awakened a sensation in Charlotte's mind. She remembered hearing it throughout the weekend they'd spent together during the conference.

Stop it. Focus!

"I'm sorry, Miles. Glad you're well. I'm okay. But I'll be a lot better if you're calling with good news."

"And by good news, do you mean—"

"Look," Charlotte interrupted. "Will you please stop stalling and tell me what's going on!"

Walter cleared his throat. She looked up, not realizing that he was still hovering in the doorway.

"Who is that?" he whispered.

She ignored him.

"All right, all right," Miles said. "I'm calling to tell you that yes, I can get the time off and come to River Valley."

Charlotte slammed her hand against the desk. "Miles! You just made me the happiest woman in the world. Thank you, thank you, thank you!"

"Miles," Walter muttered. "Who the hell is Miles?"

"Hey, hold on a sec," Charlotte said before pulling the phone away from her ear. "Corporal Kincaid, if you have anything else to discuss with me, you'll have to table it for later."

He threw her a look of irritation before taking his time walking off.

"Okay, I'm back," she said into the phone.

"Listen, Charlotte. You don't have to thank me. I'm happy to help in any way that I can."

"I'm sure you can guess my next question. How soon can you get here?"

"This weekend. I would try and make it sooner, but I've got a few case files to close out."

"Understood. I'm just glad you're coming. Do you need help booking flights or a hotel or anything?"

"No, I've got all of that taken care of. I booked a one-way ticket there since I didn't know how long you'd need me. And I'm staying at the River Valley Inn."

"Perfect. Be sure to send me your receipts so I can have the department reimburse you. Oh, and, Miles?"

"Yes?"

"I really appreciate this. I know things between us didn't end on the highest note after we met. I could've handled the situation differently. But I was in a bad place after a really bitter divorce. So… I apologize."

"Listen, I appreciate the apology. But that's old news. Let's start over fresh and just focus on the investigation."

"Point taken. Send me your trip details when you get a chance. I'll pick you up from the airport and we'll get to work as soon as you arrive. In the meantime, if there are any new developments in the case, I will let you know. I'll send you copies of the case files, too."

"Good. That'll be helpful. Talk soon."

Charlotte disconnected the call and jetted toward Chief Mitchell's office. On the way there, Walter jumped in front of her.

"Hey, what was that phone call abo—"

"I don't have time to chat, Corporal," she interrupted, brushing past him. "I've got some big news to report to the chief."

Chapter Three

Miles followed Charlotte along the shoreline of Lake Lise. He stepped cautiously across the desert floor, careful to avoid the deep cracks nestled between gravel and sand.

He'd arrived in Nevada late that morning. Thinking back on the moment he stepped off the plane, Miles chuckled to himself, remembering how his calf muscles quivered with anticipation as he made his way through Harry Reid International Airport. When he exited the terminal and laid eyes on Charlotte, the detective was hit with a flood of emotions.

She was just as stunning now as she'd been back when they first met. The way her silky black hair framed her slender face, offsetting dimpled cheeks and piercing brown eyes. Her lips, the bottom slightly fuller than the top, shimmered in her signature pale pink gloss. When they parted, he recalled how soft they'd once felt pressed against his.

He'd greeted her with a long embrace, melting into the warmth of her body. The spark was still there, shooting up his back when her hands glided across his shoulder blades. Just as he'd inhaled the rose-scented perfume pulsating from her neck, she pulled away, rushing him off to the crime scene where the first victim's body had been found.

Miles had tried to make eye contact. Read into her gaze. See if it would reveal what her words wouldn't—that she still had feelings for him. But Charlotte wasn't having it. Her nervousness was apparent, as was her avoidance.

When he'd suggested they catch up over brunch before diving into work, just to get reacquainted and iron out any awkward kinks between them, Charlotte turned him down. She wanted to get to Lake Lise well before the sun set. During the fifty-minute drive there, she'd been all business. Miles tried to interject a little small talk in between the details of the case. But Charlotte managed to avoid discussing anything personal.

Now, as they continued along the water's edge, the conversation remained solely on the investigation.

"What many people don't realize," she said, "is that there are a number of water sources throughout Nevada. Folks think of this state as some dry, barren flatland. But there are miles of lake beds flowing between these vast mountain ranges."

"It's interesting that your suspect is leaving his victims near random bodies of water in a state known for its drylands. Is he trying to send some sort of message?"

"Well, one of my colleagues thinks the Smiley Face Killer could be behind the murders. I'm not buying into that theory. There are too many differences in the cases. But I do believe our killer may have copied that aspect of the Smiley Face Killer's modus operandi."

"Why? To try and throw you off into thinking that this could be their work?"

"Could be…"

Miles watched as Charlotte skipped over a trail of eroded gray stones. Her waist twisted, causing her slim-fitting jeans to move against her curvy hips. He pressed his fingertips against his eyes and turned away.

"Well, I have to agree with you," he said. "Between what you've told me about this case and everything I've read in the files, I highly doubt that the Smiley Face Killer is behind these murders."

"I honestly think my colleague is just trying to insert himself into this investigation any way he can. *He* may not really even believe that theory. You'll understand why I say that once you meet him."

Charlotte led Miles toward a dilapidated picnic table near the edge of a seventy-foot cliff. "Here's where River Valley's first victim's body was found. Underneath the table. Her name was Brandy Graves. Twenty-five years old. Just graduated law school. She was out with her girls, celebrating a new job. Got separated from the group and went missing for twelve days."

"I remember reading her case file. Like the other victims, she had a number carved into her cheek. Eleven, if I recall correctly." Miles slowed down as they approached the table. Only two of its splintered legs were still standing. Both benches on either side were lopsided like a seesaw. "And what about the cause of death? You mentioned that there was no trauma to the bodies."

"Right." Charlotte sighed. "Which makes this case that much more complicated. There's been no viable evidence left at the crime scenes, and no obvious causes of death."

"So what are you and the medical examiner thinking? Poisoning, maybe?"

"Definitely. We're still waiting on the toxicology reports to come back. But succinylcholine is a possibility."

"Ahh, the popular muscle relaxant, better known as sux," Miles said. "That makes sense. It can cause respiratory paralysis if too much is administered, which will quickly lead to death. Plus, sux oftentimes goes undetected during autopsies."

He pulled out his cell phone and snapped several photos of the scene, then began shooting videos of the surrounding area. The camera caught a glimpse of Charlotte, watching him intently. When Miles pulled the phone down, she quickly turned away.

"You all right?" he asked, the question chased by a smile.

"Yep…yeah. I'm fine. Why?"

"No reason." He shrugged, deciding against calling her out for gawking.

"Listen, I wanna check out the other crime scene in River Valley at some point. Glacier Lake, right?"

Charlotte ran her hands up and down her arms. Despite the steamy temperature, her body appeared to shiver. "Right. But, um… Miles, there are a couple of things that I didn't share with you during our initial phone call."

"I'm listening."

"I was attacked a few weeks ago."

"You were *what*?" Miles yelled so loudly that a couple walking near the shore stopped and looked their way. "Why didn't you tell me that? I would've come here sooner had I known. Who attacked you?"

Charlotte stared down at the silver bracelet on her wrist, fiddling with the geometric-shaped charms. "I don't know. He hasn't been caught yet."

"I'm so sorry." Just as Miles raised his arms to embrace her, she fell into his chest. "Were you hurt?"

"No. Just a little banged up. And shaken up, of course."

"Sure. That's to be expected. I'm glad you're okay."

The pair slowly pulled away from one another.

"And, uh, that's not all," Charlotte continued. "I've been getting harassed, too. What started off as petty little occurrences turned into more serious threats."

"What kind of threats?"

"My car being keyed, tires being punctured, strange text messages, emails and phone calls. That type of thing. I've felt like I'm being followed, too. So, with all that happening, plus juggling my promotion and this investigation, I'm in over my head. Which is another reason why I called you here."

The look of fear in Charlotte's distant gaze sent a streak of anger through Miles.

"You already know I'm gonna do all that I can to protect you. And I'm assuming you've already reported this to the department."

"I have. But, honestly? I don't know if anyone's taking it seriously. Chief Mitchell is so focused on solving this case that I think he's let that investigation slip through the cracks. Unintentionally, of course."

"Do you have any idea who might be behind the threats?"

Charlotte expelled an exasperated sigh. "I'm thinking it could be the killer, or a jealous colleague."

"Or it could be both."

She nodded, staring out at the rippling blue water. "I've thought about that, too. That's where you come in. I need an unbiased person by my side to help figure it all out. Someone who I know will have my back."

"You already know I'll be holding you down every step of the way." Miles paused, inching closer toward her. "Can I ask you something?"

"Of course."

"Is this investigation the only reason why you called me here?"

Charlotte's lips parted, but she remained silent. Every muscle in Miles's face tensed as he stared her down.

"In all honesty," she said, "yes. If anything, I resisted at first because of our personal history, but ultimately the job is more important than that, and we're both adults."

The swell of hope that had been pounding inside his chest plummeted to the soles of his feet.

"But, full disclosure?" she continued.

"Yes. Please."

"Being in your presence again has brought back emotions that I didn't expect to feel. And... I don't quite know how to process that."

Here it is. Your second chance...

Miles took Charlotte's hand in his. Her fingers remained limp within his grasp.

"However," she began, "with that being said, I think we should keep things professional. I've gotta stay focused. As River Valley's new sergeant, not to mention first female sergeant, I can't make any missteps. The entire department is looking to me to solve this case, right along with the media and these victims' families. So, the heat is on. I've got my work cut out for me and cannot afford any distractions."

"Oh, so I'm a distraction?"

"You know what I mean, Miles. Plus, I already made the mistake of dating a coworker. That ended in disaster. Now that you and I have partnered up, I don't want history to repeat itself."

"Okay, so I'm a distraction *and* a mistake in the making. Wow." His arms fell by his sides. "This is taking me right back to when we first met. But I get it. I guess…"

Charlotte stood there silently, which Miles took to mean that the conversation was over.

"Are we done here?" he asked.

"Please tell me you're not upset."

"Upset? No. I'm just keeping it professional, per your request."

"Touché. Okay then, why don't you let me treat you to lunch, then we'll stop by the police station so you can meet the team?"

"Sounds like a plan," Miles conceded, his gait heavy with disappointment as he followed Charlotte back to the car.

Chapter Four

Charlotte and Miles walked side by side through the police station's parking lot. She peered at him from the corners of her eyes, thinking the same thoughts she'd had throughout lunch—that he had somehow grown even more handsome over the years. His dark, close-cut, wavy hair appeared thicker. His well-defined features and reddish-brown complexion were flawless, as was his toned, trim physique.

"Ready for me to meet all of your comrades?" Miles asked.

"Yep," Charlotte chirped despite feeling somewhat reluctant. "Let's do it."

The moment they entered the station, she made a beeline toward Chief Mitchell's office. Charlotte could feel everyone's eyes on them. But no one's glare was more penetrating than Walter's.

He'd been standing near the reception desk when they walked in. She held her head high and hurried past, acting as if she hadn't seen him.

Please don't try and pull a stop and chat, she'd thought. Luckily, he didn't.

During their lunch at The Capital Grille, Charlotte told Miles about her relationship with Walter. He appeared to lose his appetite, picking over his salmon Caesar salad while questioning whether she'd been in love with him. The question took Charlotte by surprise. She'd danced around a clear response.

"We, um…we were pretty close."

"Was he angry when you broke up with him?"

She hesitated, then slowly nodded. "He was."

"Is he trying to win you back?"

"He is."

"Okay, well, I guess that solves the mystery of who's been threatening you."

She didn't like to jump to the conclusion that it was Walter, but the thought had crossed her mind.

"Whoever it is, my hope is that we'll catch him soon," Charlotte said before quickly changing the subject.

And now, as the pair walked through the station, she prayed that Walter wouldn't approach them.

Miles took his time while trailing behind her, casually glancing around the department. His eyes danced inquisitively as he checked out his surroundings.

Charlotte, however, saw right through his doe-eyed curiosity. She knew he was trying to figure out which officer she'd dated.

When Walter came sauntering toward them, she held her breath, bracing herself for an awkward exchange.

"I see we've got an unfamiliar face around here," Walter said just as Chief Mitchell exited the break room.

"Hey, Chief!" Charlotte yelled, waving him down.

Chief Mitchell jumped back so abruptly that he spilled hot coffee on his hand.

"Dammit, Charlotte! You scared me. What is going on?"

She grabbed Miles's arm and pulled him toward her

boss. "My apologies. Can we please go to your office and talk? *Now?*"

Miles snorted, leaning into her ear. "I've gotta meet Walter at some point. No better time than the present, right?"

"Wrong," she hissed under her breath.

Chief Mitchell's rotund belly jiggled as he charged back inside the break room and grabbed a stack of napkins. "I've only got time for a quick chat. I have a call with the medical examiner's office in fifteen minutes." He did a double take. "Is this the detective from Clemmington you were tell—"

"I'll tell you all about it in your office," Charlotte interrupted while herding the men down the hallway. The moment they stepped inside the chief's office, she closed the door so fast that it clipped the back of Miles's shoes.

"Sorry," she muttered. "Chief Mitchell, this is Detective Miles Love. And yes, he is the investigator I've been telling you about who works for Clemmington PD. Detective Love, meet Chief Mitchell."

Miles shook his hand. "It's nice to meet you, sir. Thank you for allowing me to assist in this case."

"Thank you for being here. That was great work you and your family did back in California, catching the maniac committing all those twisted murders. Please, have a seat."

"I appreciate that. I think the case of the heart-shaped murders might be the one to send my father into retirement. Which wouldn't be a bad thing considering my mother's been wanting him to turn in his badge for the past couple of years."

"Tell her to join the club. My wife's been begging me

to retire for the past *ten* years. But…" The chief's voice trailed off as he glanced around his spacious yet cluttered office. Stacks of cardboard boxes filled with old case files lined the walls. His worn cherrywood desk had been there since the day he started, right along with the tattered, mismatched chairs surrounding it. "I'm not ready to trade all this in. Not yet. But anyway, enough about me. What's the game plan between you two?"

"Well," Charlotte said, "I've spent the afternoon catching Miles up on all the case details. We visited the crime scene out at Lake Lise, and he took plenty of photos and notes. We're planning to review the autopsy reports of the murder victims and see if anything jumps out at Miles that the department may have overlooked."

"That sounds like a good place to start," the chief said just as someone knocked on the door.

"Uh-oh," Charlotte muttered, already knowing who it was.

Walter cracked open the door and stuck his head inside. Chief Mitchell continued talking while he stood in the doorway with his mouth hanging open.

"The medical examiner is supposed to have the toxicology results back on Brad Ellington and Brandy Graves this afternoon. I'm curious to find out what'll show up, if anything. Sergeant Bowman, you should join me on that call. Detective Love, would you like to sit in on it as well?"

"I'd love to. Thanks."

"Chief," Walter interjected, "that sounds like it'll be an interesting discussion. Would you mind if I sit in on it as well?"

Chief Mitchell turned to Charlotte. "Sergeant? This

is your case, so it's your call. Did you change your mind about partnering up with Corporal Kincaid?"

Oh, hell no, she almost blurted out. "No, I did not," she replied instead. "And now that Detective Love is here to assist in the investigation, I don't think it's necessary for Corporal Kincaid to be a part of the conversation with the medical examiner. I'd prefer to limit the participants."

"Humph," Walter grunted before stepping inside the office. "Well, since things have been somewhat quiet around the station, I've been reviewing the case files. I was thinking that maybe the killer's been using GHB to poison his victims."

The room fell silent.

"You know," Walter continued, "the date-rape drug?"

"We know what GHB is," Charlotte replied through tight lips. "The medical examiner tested both victims' blood and urine during the initial autopsies. There were no traces of it found in either of their systems."

"I wasn't offering up a definition for you," he shot back before pointing at Miles. "I was doing it for your friend here. Figured he may not know what I'm talking about."

Miles turned in his chair and faced Walter. "I actually discovered that GHB, better known as gamma hydroxybutyric acid, had been ruled out early on in the investigation when I reviewed the case files myself. Charlotte and I have moved on to more sophisticated drugs of choice. Succinylcholine, perhaps, or maybe even tetrahydrozoline. Could even be propofol."

Walter shoved his hands inside his pockets while looking down his nose at the detective.

"Have you heard of those drugs, Corporal?" Chief Mitchell asked.

"Uhh, I believe I may have—"

"Are you aware of the effects they'd have on the human body if administered improperly?"

"I, umm… Actually, no, sir."

The chief glanced down at the silver watch clinging to his chubby wrist. "I'll tell you what. Why don't you go study up on those drugs while Sergeant Bowman, Detective Love and I handle the call with the medical examiner?"

Walter hesitated, his eyes narrowing while glaring at Charlotte and Miles. "Yes, sir," he finally said through clenched teeth that sent his temples pulsating. His anger was palpable as he shuffled into the hallway.

"Nice meeting you!" Miles called out.

Walter responded by slamming the door behind him.

"Looks like somebody's feelings are hurt," Chief Mitchell said.

Charlotte had already revealed her past with Miles to the chief so everything was aboveboard, and he'd said he trusted her judgment. So rather than address his comment, she pulled out her notebook and opened it to a blank page. "Oh, well. Let's get down to business, shall we?" she suggested right before the chief's phone rang.

"Here we go." He tapped the speakerphone button. "Chief Mitchell speaking."

"Good afternoon, Chief Mitchell. This is Dr. Peterson."

"Hey, Doc. I've got Sergeant Bowman and Detective Love from Clemmington, California, here with me. What have you got for us?"

"Nothing new, unfortunately. There were no positive results in Ms. Graves's and Mr. Ellington's toxicology report."

Charlotte slid her chair closer to the desk. "Hello, Dr. Peterson. So there didn't appear to be any drugs in either of the victims' systems?"

"So far, no. And that was after we analyzed their blood, urine, hair, sweat and saliva."

"Dr. Peterson, this is Detective Love speaking. Is there a more extensive analysis you could administer that would pick up traces of drugs this test may have missed? Such as succinylcholine and tetrahydrozoline, for example?"

"There is, actually. I can go back in and perform a spinal tap, then collect fluid from the victims. Hopefully that'll identify and diagnose the exact cause of death. Problem is, drugs like succinylcholine and tetrahydrozoline don't stay in the system very long, which can make them difficult to detect. But we'll see what the test results reveal."

Chief Mitchell gave Charlotte and Miles a thumbsup. "Sounds good, Doc. How long do you think it'll take to get those results back?"

"Well, in some cases, I can tell the cause of death right away depending on what comes back. But it usually takes at least forty-eight hours to get the full results."

"Please keep us posted," the chief said.

"I certainly will. As soon as I know more, I'll give you a call."

Disappointment churned inside Charlotte's stomach. She'd hoped the results would offer up some sort of information that would bring them one step closer to solving the case.

And getting this killer off my trail...

Miles slid his chair toward hers, as if sensing her distress. "In the meantime," he said, "Sergeant Bowman and I will analyze the crime scene at Glacier Lake, continue reviewing the case files and maybe visit some of the places the victims were last seen before they went missing."

"Good idea," Chief Mitchell told them. He pushed his silver bifocals toward the tip of his nose, staring at them over the rim. "While you two are at it, Sergeant Bowman, be sure to show Detective Love around River Valley so that he can get a sense of the town. Let him see some sights. Try some of our great restaurants." He pointed at Miles. "Bowman's been through a lot with this investigation. I don't want her to overdo it. And while the department is working to protect her, I'm glad you're here. There's no harm in having an extra set of eyes on my sergeant."

Miles wrapped his arm around the back of her chair. "Trust me. I will do all that I can to keep her safe."

The chief reached inside his drawer, pulled out an envelope and slid it in front of Charlotte.

"What's this?" she asked.

"A gift card to Havana's Bistro. I've been holding on to it since my birthday. Why don't you two take it and go have dinner there? Decompress over a couple of marinated steaks. Or chicken breasts baked in plantain leaves. And you've gotta try their vanilla cream caramel flan." He sat back and licked his lips. "Ooh, now I'm getting hungry. Maybe I should keep that—"

Charlotte snatched the gift card off the desk. "Don't even think about it!"

The chief stood and chuckled, pulling his cracked black leather belt over his belly. "Fine. Take it. Is there anything else you two need to discuss before I go outside for a quick smoke break?"

"Smoke break," Charlotte rebutted. "I thought you quit. Does Mrs. Mitchell know you're smoking again?"

"No, she does not. And I'd like to keep it that way. Now stop acting like the feds and get out of my office before I take back my gift card."

"Thanks, *Chief,*" Charlotte said fondly. He'd always been like a father figure to her, looking out for her when she needed it the most. For that, she would always be grateful.

"It was great meeting you, Chief Mitchell," Miles said.

"Likewise. If you two discover anything new, no matter how small, be sure to let me know. We have got to get this bastard off the street before he takes another life."

"Will do, sir."

Charlotte led Miles to her office. "Ready to look over these files and see what we can find—"

She paused when Walter came running up from behind.

"So how did the call with the medical examiner go?" he panted.

"It went well," Charlotte responded, her tone as dry as the Sahara. "Miles, would you like a bottle of water or cup of coffee before we get started?"

"I'm good for now. Thanks."

Walter hovered in the doorway, eagerly tapping his foot. "Oh, were you going to the break room? Because I can walk with you. I'd love a cup of—"

"Detective Love and I are about to get to work. So, no. I'm not going to the break room."

Walter pointed in Miles's direction. "You got the whole office buzzing about you, man. Is it even legal for a California law enforcement officer to be working a case here in Nevada?"

The detective turned to Charlotte. "Do you wanna take this one? Or should I?"

"Be my guest," she replied, her lips curling into a mischievous grin.

"Thank you. Corporal Kincaid, according to the California-Nevada Compact for Jurisdiction on Interstate Waters, law enforcement officers in both California and Nevada are allowed to arrest suspects who've committed crimes on Lake Tahoe and Topaz Lake."

Walter's head tilted as he side-eyed Miles. "Really? Huh…and, uh—where did you get this information?"

"From the Nevada State Legislature," Charlotte responded coolly. "Title 14, Chapter 171." She could sense the defeat drifting off Walter's heaving chest. *Finish him*, she thought as Miles continued.

"And I'm not sure just how much you know about this case, Corporal, but the Numeric Serial Killer's first victim was found on the shore of Lake Tahoe."

Walter snorted loudly. "Yeah, I know. Wanda Osborne. I could never forget her story."

"That is incorrect. It was actually a man named William Oglesby."

"And on that note," Charlotte said, sauntering toward

the door, "Detective Love and I need to get to work. Did you have any other questions, Corporal Kincaid?"

He rocked back on his heels, posturing as if he wanted to say more. She didn't give him the chance.

"Enjoy the rest of your afternoon," Charlotte told him before closing the door.

"That's cold," Miles said, bursting out laughing.

"Trust me. It's well deserved." She pulled several folders from her drawer and placed them in front of Miles. "Ready to get started?"

"I am. But now Chief Mitchell has me fiending for some chicken and marinated steak."

"Work now, eat later." Charlotte cracked open her laptop. "Now let's get to it."

Chapter Five

Charlotte pulled in front of the River Valley Inn. "I am absolutely stuffed. You should've stopped me at the chargrilled skirt steak and Latin fries. But *nooo*. You just sat there and watched me run wild with the sweet potato pudding!"

"At least give me credit for stopping you at one mojito since you're driving. But as for the meal? No. You deserve to indulge. I remember how strict you are with your diet. Organic this, keto that. Live a little. You look great. A comforting meal every once in a while isn't gonna hurt you," Miles insisted before glancing at his watch.

"Why do you keep checking the time? Is there somewhere you need to be?"

"No. I'm concerned about you driving home by yourself this late."

"This late? It's not even nine o'clock yet."

"I know. But it's pitch-black out here. You have to drive through some pretty deserted areas to get home, don't you?"

"I do. However, I've driven these roads thousands

of times. And my house is only fifteen minutes away. I'll be fine."

"Are you sure?"

"I'm positive. Plus, did you forget that I am a River Valley police sergeant?" Charlotte patted her purse. "And I'm carrying a loaded Glock 22?"

"No, I didn't. But did *you* forget that a serial killer is running around town who we suspect may have attacked you? Not to mention those threats you've been receiving."

"Of course I haven't forgotten. But what do you want me to do? Stay here and spend the night with you?"

Miles threw her a sly grin.

"Okay now!" She swatted his arm. "You know I didn't mean it like that."

"Look, I'm going to get a rental car tomorrow. I don't like the idea of you driving me around, then dropping me off and going home alone."

"Suit yourself."

Charlotte stared out the window. Aside from the dim yellow light shining down on the two-story inn's white brick exterior, the surrounding area was eerily dark. But knowing Miles was in town made her feel safe. News of his presence would spread. Everyone in the department already knew he was here. So if she were being harassed by a jealous colleague, Charlotte expected the threats to cease.

"I'll tell you what," Miles said. "Why don't you pick me up in the morning, we'll go have breakfast, then head to the rental car company? Tonight will be the last time you play chauffeur. It should be the other way around."

Charlotte thought back on her days of dating Walter. She'd driven them everywhere the majority of the time. He would blame wanting to ride shotgun on a bad right knee, never caring about her being behind the wheel alone late at night. She had eventually caught on to his motive—wanting to indulge in limitless cocktails.

"Thank you, Miles. I appreciate that. Pick you up at seven?"

"Sounds good. See you then. And be careful. Call me as soon as you get home."

"Yes, Dad," she joked.

Miles planted a lingering kiss on Charlotte's cheek. A rush of air seeped through her parted lips. She closed her eyes, taking in the feel of his soft, warm lips.

"Don't forget to let me know you made it in," he said before climbing out.

Charlotte watched as he headed inside. His sexy, athletic swagger had her tingling in places that she shouldn't.

Girl, go home!

Instead of following her command, she continued to sit there, ogling Miles. Right before entering the lobby, he turned and waved, then gestured for her to get moving.

"The shower will be running cold tonight," she muttered before driving off.

Dense layers of fog rolled across her windshield. Charlotte switched on the bright lights and made a right turn onto Peak Avenue. She glanced over at the empty passenger seat, already feeling the void of Miles's absence.

The urge to call him suddenly hit. Charlotte shook

it off. He was already worried that she was alone. No need to exacerbate his concern. But that wasn't the only reason. She also didn't want to appear clingy.

Charlotte switched on the satellite radio and hit channel 104. A classic Steve Harvey stand-up routine was playing. She turned up the volume, sinking into her seat as the jokes put her mind at ease.

Until a pair of headlights flashed erratically behind her.

Charlotte's head swiveled back and forth between the rearview and side-view mirrors. The billowing smog prevented her from getting a good look at the vehicle.

"Can you please get off my bumper!" she yelled, as if the driver could hear her.

The car sped up, now inches away from hers. It swerved wildly from right to left. The headlights continued to flash. Then its piercing horn blew erratically.

"What in the hell are you doing?" Charlotte screamed, tightening her grip on the wheel.

The vehicle darted over into the left lane, despite it being a two-way street. Its engine roared as the car picked up speed, quickly catching up to Charlotte.

They rode side by side. She slowed, and it slowed, so she pressed down on the accelerator while struggling not to run off the road. Charlotte reached for her phone to call Miles. But it was inside her purse, which had flown into the back seat. She contemplated lunging for it, remembering she'd yet to sync the cell with the car's Bluetooth, then reconsidered. One wrong move and she'd veer off into the desert, ending up blinded by a flurry of sand.

The car crept closer to Charlotte's. She screamed,

jerking her vehicle away from the assailant's. She skidded over the edge of the desert. A blanket of gravel enveloped her sedan. She veered back and forth, the steering wheel taking on a life of its own. The passenger side of her car rode the shoulder. The attacker's vehicle was inches away from the driver's side. He had her hemmed in. A collision was looming, unless she drove farther into the pitch-black desert.

Charlotte slammed on her brakes. The assailant zoomed down the road. She spun out of the sand and hit the accelerator, driving off in the opposite direction.

Within seconds, the assailant made a U-turn. Then suddenly, the road became crowded. Headlights flashed everywhere. Charlotte grew disoriented. But the one thing she could still make out was her attacker, back on her tail.

Charlotte sped up, weaving through the traffic until the road cleared.

"Please tell me I lost him. *Please* tell me I lost him…"

One glance in the rearview mirror proved that she hadn't. Whoever was chasing her came up the rear, then pulled up on the side. He veered toward her in yet another attempt to run her off the road. She sensed the move coming and swerved to the right, barely avoiding a collision.

I should've listened to Miles. I should not have driven home alone…

But it was too late for regrets. Charlotte had to save herself.

An eighteen-wheeler came racing down the street, heading straight toward the assailant's car. Its booming horn blared into the foggy night air.

Charlotte's attacker slammed on his accelerator, almost crashing into her.

"Get away from me!" she screamed, wiping a sheet of sweat from her forehead.

The car rammed into her bumper. Charlotte jolted forward, her head banging against the steering wheel. She moaned, sitting up slowly. Through her muddled vision, she saw the driver pull up next to her.

Find your gun! Shoot him!

A flash of silver shone off the passenger seat. Charlotte's Glock 22 must've fallen from her purse. She grabbed it and rolled down the window. Stuck her arm out and pointed the gun at the car.

The driver slammed on his brakes. He lost control and spun out in the middle of the street.

Pop!

"Good!" Charlotte yelled, hoping he'd blown out a tire. She pulled over and scrambled for her cell phone, her fingers trembling as she dialed 9-1-1.

"Nine-one-one, what is your emergency?"

"Cindy! It's Sergeant Bowman. Listen, I am on Peak Avenue near the corner of Willow and Circle Drive. Send backup. Now! I'm being chased by some lunatic."

"I'm calling for backup right now, Sergeant. Stay on the line with me. Is the assailant actively chasing you?"

"No. I pulled my gun on him and he lost control of his car. Got stuck in the middle of the road. I don't want to try and apprehend him alone, because if he's our Numeric Serial Killer, he may be heavily armed. But I'll have eyes on him until the rest of law enforcement gets here."

"Ten-four, Sergeant. Help is on the way."

Charlotte peered into the side-view mirror. Her attacker was gone.

"Wait," she uttered. "Where'd he go? Where did he go!"

She stumbled out of the car and stared down the street. It was empty.

"Dammit!"

"What's happening now, Sergeant Bowman?"

"My assailant! He…he got away. But…*how*? He'd lost control of his vehicle and blew out a tire, and…" Charlotte fell against the door, her legs weak with frustration.

"Did you get a look at the vehicle?" Cindy asked. "Or the license plate?"

"No. It's too dark and foggy out here. It looked like a dark sedan, but that's all I could make out."

"I've still got law enforcement heading your way. How are you doing? Do you need medical attention?"

Charlotte gritted her teeth and flung open her door, falling into the seat. "No. I'm okay. Tell the officers they don't have to come out here. There's no need. The man is gone."

"Well, should I at least send someone to escort you home? What if he heads back that way and finds that you're still out there?"

"He won't."

"How do you know?"

"Because he got a good look at my Glock when I pointed it directly at his car."

"Oh," Cindy replied. "Gotcha. That'll do it."

"I'm leaving the scene now. I'll check back in with

you once I make it home, and fill out a report tomorrow. Not that it'll do any good."

"Don't get discouraged. Maybe he'll be apprehended this time. But in the meantime, be careful out there."

"I will."

Charlotte disconnected the call and dialed Miles's number. He picked up on the first ring.

"Hey," he said. "I was just thinking about you. It's been more than fifteen minutes since you dropped me off. Did you take the long way home?"

"I never made it home. Pack an overnight bag. I'm heading back to the inn to pick you up. You're staying with me tonight. If you don't mind," she quickly added.

There was a long pause on the other end of the phone.

"Do you mind?" Charlotte asked.

"No. Of course not. I just— This is so unexpected, that's all. What happened to make you want me to stay the night?"

"It's a long story. I'll explain everything when I get there."

Chapter Six

Miles sat at Charlotte's white marble kitchen island, watching as she cleared their plates.

"I would've been happy to take you out to breakfast, you know," he told her.

"I know. I wasn't in the mood to sit down at a restaurant and be seen in public. But thank you for offering. And for staying here with me last night. I really appreciate it."

"You don't have to thank me. That's why I'm here. To help you in any way I can. So if it means getting homemade scrambled cheese eggs, extra crispy turkey bacon, perfectly toasted bagels and a delicious cup of cappuccino, then hey, I'm all in."

Charlotte pulled a lock of hair behind her long, delicate neck and smiled softly. "Thanks. Glad you enjoyed it."

"You're welcome. Can I help you clean up?"

"Absolutely not. Sit back and enjoy your coffee. You've done enough just by being here."

Miles reclined against the back of his gray suede stool, watching Charlotte as she fluttered about the kitchen. She could be so tough, yet she had a gentle way about her that he found extremely appealing. The way her slender fingers wrapped around the glasses, and her lithe legs moved gracefully as she went back and forth between the island and the sink. Not to mention the sweet scent of her vanilla and lavender lotion wafting through the air.

Charlotte's three-story townhome was glamorous yet homey with its plush neutral furnishings, fur rugs and colorful abstract artwork. Framed photographs of her family and friends were scattered around the house, as were exotic souvenirs she'd collected while vacationing over the years.

I could get used to this, Miles thought as he plucked a grape from a midnight blue Murano glass bowl.

"A memento from Venice," she'd said earlier when he mentioned the dish's beauty.

Being in Charlotte's presence made him realize that his feelings for her never waned. If anything, they were even stronger this time around.

When she bent down to pick up a napkin that had fallen to the floor, Charlotte's pink romper rose toward the top of her thighs. Miles turned away, knowing that if he kept looking, something of his might rise as well.

Her phone pinged. She hopped up and tapped the screen, then burst out laughing.

"What's so funny?"

She handed him the phone. "Check out this text message Cindy just sent me."

Char, you won't believe this. Word around the station is that Walter's pissed you brought in an outsider to assist in the serial killer investigation. So now he's planning to single-handedly make an arrest so that HE can be the hero and win you back. LOL!

Miles didn't find the message amusing. It was actually quite annoying.

"Walter is such a clown," Charlotte said.

Couldn't have said it better myself, Miles thought. But he kept the comment to himself. He didn't want to appear petty or as if he was in competition to win Charlotte back.

He set her phone on the island, drained his cup and stood. "I guess we should head to the station."

"I was thinking we could stop by Glacier Lake first. I want you to check out that crime scene. See if anything sticks out at you—"

Her cell phone pinged again.

"Ugh," Charlotte groaned. "I don't wanna hear about Walter anymore, Cindy."

She read the text, then dropped her phone. It crashed onto the island. Miles jumped at the loud thump.

"What's wrong now?" he asked. "Did Walter say something even more irritating than he did in the first message?"

Charlotte didn't utter a word. She just stood there shaking, staring at Miles through watery eyes.

He hurried around the island and wrapped his arm around her. Her skin was covered in goose bumps.

"What is going on?" he asked.

"Chief Mitchell just texted me. We've got another murder on our hands."

Miles grabbed her cell and scanned the message.

I need for you and Det. Love to get to the Hoptree River ASAP! Stephen Seymour's body was found near the shore this morning. Considering he's the district

attorney's son, this is going to be a high-profile case.
The media is already out there. Let me know when
you're on the way.

"Oh no..." He tried to hand her the phone. She turned
away.

"I can't," Charlotte murmured. "Not yet."

"I got you," Miles said before sending a response.
As he typed, Charlotte leaned into him, her body trembling against his.

"I can barely process one murder before another one
is committed," she whispered into his chest.

"I know. But I'm here now. So together, we're gonna
go hard and do whatever it takes to catch this bastard."
He pulled away and raised her chin, staring directly into
her eyes. "Come on. You're good. Take a deep breath,
regroup, and let's get to the crime scene."

MILES AND CHARLOTTE walked along the shoreline of the
Hoptree River. He looked out at the crisp blue water, its
calm waves washing over colorful rocks and course tan
sand. Lush greenery grew from the majestic cliffs bordering the lake. Docks housed sleek motorboats and jet
skis. And now, yellow caution tape blocked off a good
portion of the area.

The river would've normally been bustling with visitors. But instead, it was swarming with law enforcement officers.

The medical examiner stood over Stephen's body,
frantically scribbling notes in a pad. Crime scene photographers took pictures of the victim. A forensic investigator slowly moved about the area, searching for

evidence. Policemen stood guard over several news outlets, who'd been relegated to the back of the crime scene. Chief Mitchell was in the near distance, holding his head while talking on the phone.

"How are you feeling?" Miles asked Charlotte.

"Good. No fear. I'm in sergeant mode now, ready to take over."

"That's my girl."

Charlotte pulled a box of latex gloves and shoe covers out of her duffel bag. She and Miles slipped them on, then made a beeline toward Chief Mitchell.

"Okay," the chief said into the phone. "Again, I am so sorry for your loss, sir. My sergeant, who's heading up the investigation, just arrived on the scene. Trust me, we're doing everything we can to catch this killer. Yes, I will absolutely keep you posted. I'll be in touch soon."

The normally cool head of River Valley PD appeared pale and discombobulated. Streams of sweat ran down his temples. His jittery hands were clenching in and out of tight fists.

"Glad you two are here," he grumbled in Charlotte and Miles's direction. "That was Thomas Seymour. Stephen's father. I really feel for that man. He lost his wife to cancer a few years back, and his oldest daughter in a car accident last year. And now," he choked out, pointing over at Stephen's body, "*this*."

"Chief Mitchell," Charlotte said, "I promise we're going to step up this investigation and catch the killer. Stephen will be our last victim. Trust me on that."

"Good. That's what I want to hear. And just so you know, the number four was carved into Stephen's left cheek."

"Had he been reported missing?" Miles asked.

"No, which is strange. His father could barely talk, so I didn't wanna ask too many questions. I figured he'd be in a better position to speak to me once a little time passes by."

"Let's hope." Charlotte ran her hand along the back of her neck as it burned under the hot sun. "I'm going to take a look at the body. Miles, can you join me?"

"Of course."

They approached the victim. Stephen's body lay peacefully in the sand, as if he'd positioned himself there to take a nap. His arms were down by his sides. His skin had turned a shade of purplish blue, while small blisters covered his legs. Stephen's white denim shorts and pale blue T-shirt were spotless. He wasn't wearing shoes, and the bottoms of his feet were completely clean.

"No bloating," Miles said. "Looks like he's only been dead about a day or so."

"I agree. There doesn't appear to be much decomposition to the body at all. Looks like somebody carefully placed him in this spot, too. My guess is that he was carried out here, hence the dirt-free feet."

The forensic investigator circled the body, studying the ground while collecting samples. "Sergeant Bowman, I've found some pretty decent evidence. There was a glass bottle and a pair of sunglasses stuck in the sand near the victim. The gravel I gathered may contain biological evidence. I'll head to the crime lab as soon as I'm done and turn everything over for testing."

"Great. Thanks, Virgil. Let's hope they can pull some DNA from it. Fingerprints, blood, sweat, saliva, *some-*

thing. Can you ask the lab director to put a rush on that analysis?"

Virgil sealed a plastic bag filled with sand. "I'm already one step ahead of you, Sarge. I called down to the lab on the way here and told the director to clear her schedule. She knows how important it is to get this case solved. So she's already expecting me."

"Awesome. Thanks."

Miles pointed over at the herd of reporters shouting questions and shoving microphones at law enforcement from behind the caution tape. "The media is in a complete frenzy."

"After word gets out about this murder, the entire town will be. I can literally feel the pressure to catch the killer closing in on me like cement walls." She turned to the medical examiner. "Dr. Peterson, thank you for getting here so quickly. Any initial thoughts on the cause of death?"

"It looks very similar to the other victims. No apparent trauma. The body is well-preserved. And there's that infamous number carved into his cheek."

"Are you thinking this victim was drugged, like the others?"

"I am."

Charlotte slipped a surgical mask over her nose and mouth and hovered over Stephen's body. "Have you performed the spinal taps on the other two victims and had their cerebrospinal fluid tested yet?"

"I have. The first round of toxicology reports came back inconclusive. So I told the lab to run them again. I'm still waiting on those results."

An earsplitting scream ricocheted through the air.

Charlotte leapt to her feet and grabbed hold of Miles, watching as a young woman charged toward them. Her curly blond ponytail flew through the air, while mascara-stained tears streaked her face.

Law enforcement stopped her just as she came crashing into the caution tape.

"Where's Stephen?" she shrieked. Where's *Stephen*?"

"Ma'am, please stand back!" one of the officers insisted.

"Should we go and find out who that is?" Miles asked Charlotte.

"Yes, we should."

The woman locked eyes with Charlotte as they approached.

"Hey! Can you *please* help me?" the woman begged. "I think that's my boyfriend over there!"

"What is your boyfriend's name?"

"Stephen. Stephen James Seymour. My cousin is a news reporter, and she just called and told me his body was found out here. Is it him? Please tell me it isn't him..."

Charlotte reached for the woman's hand. "I am so sorry."

"Stephen's *dead*?" she wailed, collapsing against Charlotte and almost knocking her down. Miles steadied them both.

"What is your name, ma'am?" he asked softly.

"Phoebe Daniels. Stephen's soon-to-be fiancée. He was my everything. *Everything*. We were gonna get married. Soon! I mean, as soon as he stopped with all the partying. That's what probably took him out, you know. The partying..."

Charlotte allowed Phoebe past the caution tape. She and Miles led her over to a nearby picnic table. Miles pulled out his notebook while Charlotte began questioning her.

"When was the last time you saw Stephen?" she asked.

"About a week ago. I begged him to stay home that night, too. But he insisted on going out with his boys."

"Do you know where they went?"

"Probably to every single bar on Rush Street."

Miles looked up from his notebook. "Where is Rush Street?"

"You must not be from around here," Phoebe said.

"He isn't," Charlotte told her before turning to Miles. "Rush Street is one of the most popular strips in downtown River Valley. It's where the majority of the town's bars and clubs are located."

"And it can get wild," Phoebe added. "Especially on a Saturday night."

"So Stephen went out with his friends last Saturday?" Miles asked.

Her eyes fell to the ground as she tapped her fingertips against her chin. "Yes. Last Saturday for sure. He left the apartment at around eight o'clock. And that was the last time I saw him—"

Her voice broke. As she sobbed into her hands, Miles leaned into Charlotte. "Last Saturday was exactly five days ago," he whispered.

She nodded and ran her hand along the left side of her face. They were on the same page. The number four that had been carved into Stephen's cheek represented the number of days between him being kidnapped and murdered.

"So it only took a day for his body to be found," she whispered. "We'll see what Dr. Peterson says once the autopsy results come in, confirming the exact date of death."

Phoebe sniffled, wiping her eyes with the neckline of her yellow tank top. "You know, I figured Saturday would be a wild night for Stephen and his friends. Every time they get together, things get outta hand. But who knew it would lead to his death?"

"Why didn't you report him missing to the authorities?" Miles asked. "Or anyone else for that matter?"

"Because Stephen was a party boy. Everybody knew that about him, including his own family. He'd go off on binges for days without contacting any of us. I figured he'd show back up at some point, just like he always did. But not this time. Because he...he was dead!"

Charlotte patted her back. "I am so sorry, Phoebe."

"Don't be sorry. Just catch this killer!"

"We're working on it."

"Well, work harder!"

"We will," Charlotte replied calmly. "I promise. Now, can you give us the names of Stephen's friends who he was with that night?"

Phoebe stared out into the distance, her eyes bulging as her body shook. Charlotte followed her gaze. The coroner had begun swabbing Stephen's fingernails.

"I can't look at that," Phoebe said, covering her mouth as she spun around on the bench. She moaned while taking in a rush of air. *"You can do this. You can do this,"* she muttered to herself before pivoting toward

Charlotte. "Okay, Stephen was out with his best friend, Hunter Stout. And Rob Lee, who's another close friend. And Josh. Josh…" Phoebe pulled out her cell phone and scrolled through the contacts. "Josh Tillman. Those are the three guys who he always hung out with. They probably met up with other people at some point, but you should start with them."

"And the bars?" Charlotte asked. "Are there any particular ones that they frequented often?"

"Absolutely. The Blue Lagoon, Eden's Den, and The Bottomless Bar. But Stephen and his friends like to bar-hop. So if I were you, I'd check the surveillance footage at every single spot on Rush Street."

A commotion ensued near Stephen's body. The autopsy technicians were placing him inside of a body bag.

Phoebe screamed, bolting from the table. "Wait! I wanna see him before you take him away!"

Charlotte gently clutched her arm. "Hold on, Phoebe. Calm down. Trust me, you do not want to see him like that. The best thing you can do for Stephen is stay put and answer our questions."

She slouched back down onto the bench, burying her head into the table just as Chief Mitchell approached.

"Sergeant Bowman, Detective Love, can I speak with you two? Privately?"

Charlotte patted Phoebe's shoulder. "Give us a sec, sweetie. We'll be right back."

She responded with a nod, her head still tucked away in her arm.

"Listen," the chief said once they were out of earshot, "Dr. Peterson is going to perform the autopsy on Stephen's body as soon as they get to the morgue. If there's a drug in his system that dissipates quickly, I'm hoping the rush will improve our chances of detecting it."

"Good," Charlotte said. "Are you satisfied with the amount of evidence that forensics collected?"

"I am. Are you?"

"Yes. And Virgil's already contacted the lab to ask that they put a rush on the DNA analysis. So hopefully we'll be getting some answers soon."

"That would be great," Chief Mitchell grunted, clawing at the red splotches covering his forearms.

"Here we go with the stress flare-up." Charlotte reached inside of her duffel bag, pulled out a bottle of oat serum and handed it to him. "Here. Try some of this."

"Did my wife tell you to pack this for me?"

"She sure did. Mrs. Mitchell knows how tense you get. Especially when we visit crime scenes."

"That woman," he griped, slathering it over his skin. He nodded in Phoebe's direction. "Who's that young lady?"

"Her name is Phoebe Daniels. She's Stephen's girlfriend."

"Poor thing. Must be tough, seeing him out here like this. Was she able to provide any pertinent information?"

"She was," Miles replied. "The last time she'd seen Stephen was Saturday night, before he went to hang out with a group of friends on Rush Street."

"Humph. Interesting…"

"Miles and I are going to stop by the bars they visited and view the surveillance footage, then call the friends in for questioning."

Charlotte crossed her fingers behind her back as she spoke. She'd interviewed friends and family of the other victims, and it had never turned up any good leads. She had a feeling about this one, though, that she might find a thread....

Chief Mitchell gave them a thumbs-up. "Good plan." He wiggled the bottle of serum in the air. "I'd better hold on to this. I don't see the day getting any less stressful for me."

Footsteps pounded behind the group. Miles and Charlotte glanced over their shoulders, rolling their eyes simultaneously at the sight of Walter.

"Sorry I'm late, sir," the corporal panted while dusting sand off his navy slacks.

"Who called you here, Kincaid?" Chief Mitchell asked. "I thought I instructed you to stay back and keep an eye on things at the station."

"Well, I, uh—I figured you all could use some extra help. When the DA's son turns up dead, it's all hands on deck, right? We've gotta get this case solved. And it looks to me that the investigation is dragging, so—"

"Chief Mitchell," Charlotte interrupted, "Detective Love and I are going to head over to Rush Street now." She grabbed Miles's arm and slowly backed away. "We'll keep you posted."

"Wait, what's happening on Rush Street?" Walter asked.

"That's where my boyfriend was last seen before he went missing!" Phoebe yelled from the picnic table.

Walter stepped in front of Miles. "Sergeant Bowman, I know that area well. *Very* well. It's my stomping ground. Why don't I go with you? We can tag team the bar owners and review surveillance footage together, just like we used to."

"I've got a better idea," Miles interjected, pushing past him. "Why don't you fall back, and let us—"

"Hold on, hold on." Chief Mitchell pulled the men apart. "I've got the *best* idea. Sergeant Bowman, Detective Love, you two go on. Talk to the bar owners. View the footage. See what you can find. Corporal Kincaid, since you're here now, why don't you help me clear the crime scene?"

"But shouldn't I be a more *active* part of this investigation?" Walter huffed defiantly.

"Corporal, that's an order!" the chief barked.

Walter's eager expression crumpled into a frown as he stormed off toward the forensics team.

"What about Phoebe?" Charlotte asked Chief Mitchell.

"I'll take care of her. You two just go and get me some evidence."

Chapter Seven

Charlotte approached The Blue Lagoon's foggy glass door and glanced inside. All the lights were out. Unoccupied dark wooden chairs were pushed neatly beneath the tables. Sunlight bounced off the mirror hanging behind the bar, highlighting dusty glasses and bottles of alcohol.

"Looks like they're closed," she said to Miles. "Should we knock anyway?"

"Might as well. Maybe the manager's hiding out in the back."

She tapped on the window. No answer. She tried again, a little harder this time. Still no answer. They waited a few minutes, then moved on.

"Why don't we try The Bottomless Bar since it's just a couple of doors down," Charlotte suggested before leading the way.

The charming, old-school street, known for its red-brick road, once housed cozy diners and specialty shops. But as River Valley's tourism grew, so did the mayor's desire to collect vacationers' dollars. Bakeries and barbershops were replaced with bars, twenty-four-hour fast-food restaurants and boutique hotels. The winding Rush

Street had transformed into a mini Las Vegas Strip, minus the casinos. Both Nevada residents and visitors were known to frequent the town for the water adventures, live music and cheap, well-crafted cocktails.

The Bottomless Bar's blacked-out windows and steel metal door prevented Charlotte from seeing inside. She crossed her fingers, hoping someone would answer as Miles banged on the door. After several seconds, it cracked open.

"Closed!" a deep voice croaked from the other side.

"Sir, it's Sergeant Bowman with the River Valley PD. I need to ask you a few questions. May I please come in?"

The door swung open. Charlotte jumped back at the sight of the man standing before them. He was at least six foot five, with biceps as big as thighs and a snarl that rivaled a pit bull's.

"Good afternoon, Sergeant," he boomed, rubbing his tattooed hand over his bald head. "What can I do for you?"

"Good afternoon. Detective Love and I are working a homicide investigation and need to take a look at your surveillance footage from last Saturday."

"Is this about the DA's son, Stephen? Wasn't he found floating in the middle of Lake Tahoe, butt naked and high on cocaine?"

"Where in the world did you hear all that?" Miles asked.

The man sized Miles up with a smirk that revealed his missing front teeth. "You must not be from around here. Word travels fast in this town."

"Yeah, well, it also travels incorrectly," the detective rebutted. "Nothing you just said is true."

Charlotte grabbed the edge of the door. "I'm sorry, what's your name?"

"Menace. And before you ask, yes. That's what my mama named me."

Fitting, Charlotte thought.

"Okay, Menace. Nice to meet you. May we please come in and take a look at that footage?"

He backed away slowly and held open the door. "Sure. But I can tell you now, you won't find anything that useful. As soon as I heard Stephen was murdered, I remembered seeing him here last weekend and reviewed the footage myself. I was a private investigator before I started managing this place. Investigative work is in my blood. So I couldn't help but to check the surveillance and see what I could uncover."

Charlotte and Miles stepped inside the dark bar. Black cement walls surrounded black tile flooring. Everything was black, from the steel tables and chairs to the bar and leather stools.

The CCTV equipment was set up behind a DJ booth. The pair watched as Menace played around on the computer, double-clicking the mouse until footage of bar patrons appeared on the screen.

"So you did see Stephen here last Saturday night?" Charlotte asked.

"Yep. He got here right before midnight and wasn't around for long. But I'll tell you this. While he was here? That kid drank his ass off. And I'm not just talking beer. He and his boys were downing silver bullets for about twenty minutes straight."

"Silver bullets?" Miles asked. "What are those?"

"They're shooters, also known as mixed shots that contain gin and scotch.

"Whew!" Charlotte breathed. "I could pass out from the thought of drinking a lethal combo like that."

"Tell me about it," Menace quipped. "Don't let my burly stature fool you. I may be all brawn, but even I have my limits. And a silver bullet is where the buck stops for me. I don't know how those guys were even able to walk out of here." He paused. "Well, actually they weren't walking. They were stumbling. Especially Stephen. He went crashing into one of the windows on the way out. I thought I was gonna have to call an ambulance. But he swore he was okay and left, bloody nose and all."

"Oh, boy," Charlotte uttered, thinking about how Stephen's father would feel once he learned all of this.

"Do you have cameras set up to record the exterior of the bar?" Miles asked.

"I do. And as for the night Stephen was here, that's where the footage gets interesting. *After* they left. Just watch." Menace pointed at the screen. "Okay, here we go. Do you see Stephen? He's right there, doing shots with his boys."

Charlotte studied the group of men. "I do see him. And he looks to be dressed in the exact same outfit he was wearing when his body was found."

"Mmm," Miles muttered, "he sure is."

The pair watched as Stephen and his friends downed drinks, grabbed women and danced around wildly.

"Just so you know," Menace said, "Stephen stopped

by The Blue Lagoon before he came here. So he was already pretty drunk when he walked through the door."

Charlotte pulled a thumb drive out of her bag and handed it to Menace. "Would you mind saving a copy of that footage for me?"

"No problem." He slid the device inside the USB port, then poked the monitor so hard that it almost toppled over. "Look! Here we go. Stephen and his friends are about to leave."

"Wow," Miles said. "You were right. Stephen can barely walk. He's bumping into almost everybody he passes."

"And his friends can't help him because they can barely stay on their own two feet," Charlotte added.

Menace enlarged the screen that highlighted the outside of the bar. "Now watch. Stephen and his friends are gonna cross the street and get in line at Eden's Den. Then Josh approaches the door and talks to the bouncer. He's probably asking if they can skip the line. The bouncer checks out the friends and nods. Josh signals them over."

Charlotte's eyes narrowed. "Okay, now they're all going inside." She paused. "Wait, go back."

Menace rewound the footage a few seconds. "You saw correctly. Stephen never entered the bar. Just Josh, Hunter and Rob."

"When you replay the video," Miles said, "first we see two of the friends practically carry Stephen toward the back of the line. Then they're out of frame. Josh talks to the bouncer and waves the guys over. Two of them show up. But Stephen doesn't."

"Exactly," Charlotte said. "Where did he go?"

Menace paused the tape and spun around. "That's the million-dollar question. When I watched the footage earlier, I saw that he never reappeared. He must've wandered off, then met with foul play, obviously."

"Are you sure he never came back into the frame?" Charlotte asked.

"Positive. And my guess is that the other guys were so drunk they didn't notice he wasn't with them."

"We need to talk to someone at Eden's Den," Charlotte told Miles. "Find out if anyone saw Stephen show up there at some point during the night."

"Hold on." Menace jotted something down on a napkin before handing it to her. "This is the owner of Eden's Den's number. Her name is Sasha. She should be able to help you."

Charlotte stood on her tippy toes and stared across the street. "I wonder if she's there now."

"Not yet. She drove to Vegas this morning to check out the nightclub and bar convention. She won't be back in River Valley until later tonight. But give her a call anyway. She can connect you with the manager, Bronson. He's usually around every Saturday and may have seen something that night."

Miles shook Menace's hand. "We can't thank you enough, man. You've been a huge help."

"Anytime." He pulled the thumb drive from the computer and handed it to Charlotte. "I want this killer off the street just as bad as everybody else."

"We're getting closer," Charlotte replied, following him to the front of the bar. "I can feel it."

"Good luck."

A blast of hot, dry air hit Charlotte and Miles the

moment they stepped outside. They sauntered up and down the street, peering inside windows and knocking on doors. No one answered.

"Looks like the only help we're gonna get here today is from Menace," Miles said.

"Why don't we head back to the station? We can debrief with Chief Mitchell, make sure the evidence was submitted to the crime lab, and put in calls to Sasha and to Stephen's friends."

"Let's do it. The challenge will be getting all that done without being bombarded by Walter."

"One can only hope…"

CHARLOTTE HUNG UP the phone and stared across her desk at Miles. "So, Eden's Den is a dead end."

"Stephen didn't show up in any of their surveillance footage?"

"According to Bronson, no."

"Well," Miles said, "we should still take a look at the video when he sends it over."

"We definitely will. I'll have Officer Haney contact the other businesses on Rush and see if any of their cameras captured Stephen entering their establishments or walking past them."

There was a knock at the door.

"Come in!" Charlotte called out.

Virgil stuck his head inside. "Sorry to interrupt. I just saw your text. I did drop the evidence off at the lab. The director has already submitted everything for processing."

"Excellent—" Charlotte paused when she heard rubber soles screeching along the floor outside of her office.

"Excuse me," Walter said, peering over Virgil's shoulder.

Virgil ignored the interruption. "Do you need anything else on my end, Sergeant?"

"No. You're good. Thank you for everything today. Awesome work."

"Thanks. If I hear anything from the lab, I'll let you know."

He could barely make his way out of the office as Walter hovered in the doorway.

"Here we go," Miles muttered.

Walter didn't wait for an invitation before stepping inside. "What's up, Sarge?"

"How can I help you, Corporal?"

His back stiffened. "May I sit?"

Charlotte held up her hand just as he reached for a chair. "Actually, Detective Love and I are in the middle of contacting witnesses. Do you need something?"

"Do *you* need something is a better question. I overheard Chief Mitchell talking to Stephen's girlfriend, Phoebe, back at the crime scene. She mentioned a few of the friends Stephen was out with the night he went missing. Hunter, Rob and Josh? I play softball with those guys. I know 'em real well. I can get any information that you want outta them. Just as long as you reconsider partnering with me on this case."

A shooting pain exploded inside Charlotte's head. She closed her eyes, wishing there were a trapdoor in the floor for Walter to fall through.

"Listen, Corporal Kincaid," Miles said. "Sergeant Bowman has had a long day. Why don't you report back once you actually speak with Stephen's friends—"

"Excuse me," Walter interrupted, "but who are you again? And why are you even addressing me? I was talking to the sergeant of the *River Valley* Police Department. You know, the one that you have absolutely no jurisdiction over?"

"Corporal Kincaid!" Charlotte said, slamming her hand against the desk. "First of all, show some respect. Second of all, as an officer of this department, you are obligated to assist in the investigation however you can. Third of all, you cannot blackmail me into doing anything. Keep this up and I will file a formal complaint against you. Is that understood?"

Walter's frontal vein protruded from his forehead. "Whatever you say," he muttered. "You know, this promotion really changed you." Just as he turned to walk away, Chief Mitchell approached.

"Bad news," the chief said. "I just got a call from Freelain & Associates. All of Stephen's friends have lawyered up. They've refused to come in for questioning. So, time to come up with a new strategy."

"Oh," Walter breathed, his lips spreading into an arrogant smirk. "Is that so?" He wiggled a finger at Charlotte. "That changes things, now doesn't it? Let me know if you wanna partner—*oops*—I mean team up with me when I go talk to Stephen's friends."

Before Charlotte could respond, Walter strutted off.

"What was that all about?" Chief Mitchell asked. "Does Corporal Kincaid know Stephen's friends personally or something?"

"That remains to be seen, sir," Charlotte said. "In the meantime, I'll put in a call to Freelain & Associates. See if I can talk the attorneys into bringing their clients in for a chat."

Chapter Eight

"I really needed this night," Charlotte said.

Miles nodded. "Same here. Glad we decided to kick back and have some downtime."

He and Charlotte were sitting out on her spacious wraparound deck, grilling snapper and corn on the cob. She'd had a mini meltdown that afternoon when Stephen's friends refused to come in for questioning, despite her pleas to their attorneys. Miles suggested they call it a day and offered to cook her dinner. She agreed without hesitation.

Charlotte refilled their glasses of pinot grigio. "I really wish we could have talked to Stephen's friends before they lawyered up. They probably would've been a lot more open and vocal. What do they have to hide?"

"Good question. We'll find out once they agree to talk to us. If they do…"

"Can you imagine Walter making that happen before I do? We'd never hear the end of it."

Miles turned the fish, then took a long drink of wine. "Well, if he's the one to pull information out of them that'll lead us to the killer, I'm sure we can find a way to endure his boasting."

"Very true. He better not mess things up, though. What if one of the friends is connected to the killer? That testimony might get tossed if Walter gets it without their attorney present." Charlotte tapped her fingernails against her glass and stared up at the sky. The sun was setting behind stunning layers of lavender and orange clouds. "It's getting a little chilly out here. Should we light the firepit?"

"Sure. That would be nice."

She grabbed the torch lighter and tinder, then stood over the circular bronze pit, her yellow sundress blowing in the wind. The breeze pulled her dress forward, silhouetting every curve of Charlotte's shapely figure.

Look away, a voice inside Miles's head spoke a moment too late. While he was still ogling her, their eyes met. Hers danced with amusement. He'd been caught.

Miles quickly turned away, closing the grill, then switching on the deck's heat lamps. "These should help warm you up, too," he blurted, his voice cracking with embarrassment.

"They will. Thank you."

He spun around just as she reached for her chair. They collided, his shoulder brushing against her breasts. Miles grabbed her before she went tumbling to the floor.

"I'm so sorry!" he breathed, his arms wrapped around her waist. "Are you okay?"

Charlotte nodded. "I'm fine."

Her gaze traveled from his lips to his neck, down to his chest. Miles moved in closer. Ran his hands down the curve of her back and rested them on her hips. Charlotte's body pressed against his. A stirring deep in his stomach pushed him to go further. He lifted her chin.

Their lips touched. Miles savored the lushness of her kiss as vanilla-flavored gloss lingered on his tongue.

Just as his hands slid down farther, the doorbell rang. Charlotte pulled away from his grasp.

"Who is that?" she panted, straightening her dress. "I'm not expecting anybody."

"I've got a surprise for you."

"You've got a what?"

"A surprise!"

Miles hurried inside the house, leaving a baffled Charlotte standing on the deck. A few moments later, he returned with someone hiding behind him.

"Who is that?" she asked.

A woman hopped out and charged toward her.

"Ella!" Charlotte screamed, embracing her sister. "When did you get to River Valley?"

"I just drove in from Reno. Came straight here after my assignment ended at Saint Mary's Hospital. They'd been short on nurses in the neonatal unit for weeks but recently brought on a few new hires. So, I've finally got some time off in between gigs."

"I am so happy to see you. You have no idea how much I need you here right now."

"I heard. A little birdie reached out and told me that you could use a little pick-me-up."

"Oh, I wonder who that could've been," Charlotte said, giving Miles a wink. "How did you manage to pull this off without me knowing?"

"Easy. I looked Ella up on Facebook and sent her a private message asking if she could come see you."

Charlotte gave his arm a gentle squeeze. "Thank you." She turned to Ella and spun her around. "You look good, girl. Your skin is glowing, your curls are luscious, your curves are curving. What's his name?"

"Now, what does me looking good have to do with a man?" Ella asked, wiggling her hips joyfully in her fitted denim dress. "Maybe I'm happy because I'm single."

"Well, if I had been dating that ex of yours, Nate, then I'd be a happy single woman, too. I was *so* glad when you two broke up."

Ella rolled her eyes. "Here we go. Number one, his name is Noel. And number two, he wasn't that bad. Just a little overbearing. And needy."

"And number three," Charlotte said, "if you add controlling and insecure, you'd be on point."

"Ha!" Ella poured herself a glass of wine and sat on the edge of a teal deck chair. "Well, none of that matters anymore. I listened to my big sis and broke things off with him—"

"*After* she found out he'd been cheating on her," Charlotte added, pointing in Miles's direction. *"She's always had bad taste in men..."*

He kept his eyes on the fish searing on the grill. "I'm staying out of this one. I do not get involved in disagreements among siblings. Including my own."

"As you should considering my sister's being overly dramatic," Ella said. "Anyway, Noel and I only dated for a few months, so it wasn't hard to move on. Now that I've dismissed The Cling-On as Charlotte used to call him, I'm happy, loving my job as a traveling nurse and enjoying an active, healthy dating life."

"Yeah, thanks to me." Charlotte began before Miles nudged her. "I pretty much orchestrated that breakup."

Miles brought the food over to the table. "Listen, why don't we give Ella a break and eat?"

"Good idea," Ella said. "Otherwise, my big sis would never let up."

As the group prepared their plates, Ella reset the conversation and threw Charlotte in the hot seat.

"So," Ella began, "enough about me, sissy poo. What's going on between you and Miles?"

Charlotte choked on a mouthful of corn while a piece of snapper fell from Miles's fork.

"What do you mean?" she asked. "We're working on this investigation together. You know that."

"Is that all you two are working on?"

"Yes," Charlotte confirmed, shooting her sister a look of death. "Now drop it, will you?"

"Okay, okay. No need to get snippy. Speaking of the investigation, what's the latest on it?"

"We're making progress," Miles said. "Slowly but surely."

"I heard about the DA's son being murdered. That was a shocker."

Charlotte set her fork down, her upbeat demeanor fading. "It was. But more evidence was recovered from that crime scene than any of the others. We're hoping something will come of it, and in the meantime, just trying to remain optimistic."

"Is that ass clown you used to date still trying to take over the case? What was his name, *Falter*?

"Wait, wait," Miles sputtered. "I almost spit out my wine. What did you call him?"

"Falter," Charlotte snorted. That's her nickname for Walter."

"It sure is. Because he was a misstep. Am I wrong?"

"Not to criticize my girl's judgment or anything," Miles said, "but no. You are not wrong at all."

"See," Ella said, "I'm not the only one in the family with a questionable dating history…"

"Listen, you two are not about to sit here and chastise me over a relationship that didn't work out. Especially when you both live in glass houses."

"Wait, why are you dragging Miles into this?" Ella asked.

"Yeah," he chimed in, clutching his chest innocently. "How did I get involved? I'm Finland. Switzerland. *Neutral* when it comes to all this drama."

"Oh, please," Charlotte snorted. "Don't sit here and play coy. I remember a few dating disasters you told me about when we first met. Remember the woman who tried to talk you into having a threesome with her and her husband? And you didn't even know she was married? Or what about the one who—"

"All right, all right." Miles waved his white napkin in the air. "I surrender. Can we please get back to Falter—I mean Walter?"

Ella cackled, pinching Charlotte's arm. "I like this guy."

"Yeah," Charlotte replied, locking eyes with Miles. "I do, too…"

His mouth went dry from her response. Rapid-fire questions flew through his mind. Had he heard her correctly? Did she just profess her feelings for him? Was it just a friend thing, or something more?

Gotta be more than friends. She did just kiss me…

Miles waited to see if she'd say more. Instead, Charlotte turned her attention back to Ella.

"As for Walter, he's as obnoxious as ever. Butting into the investigation, trying to partner up with me, trying to take it over."

"Hating on me," Miles added. "Trying to win Charlotte back…"

"Which will never happen," she quipped. "But anyway, we found out that Walter hangs out with a few of Stephen Seymour's friends. Which is weird."

"Very weird," Ella said. "Those guys are at least ten years younger than him. Can you say early midlife crisis? I'm telling you, Char, that man hasn't been right since you broke up with him. I've always thought he was the one behind those threats you've been getting. And to hear that he's connected to Stephen and his friends? That's suspicious."

"So what are you saying?" Miles asked. "That Walter might have something to do with Stephen's murder?"

"Yes," Ella confirmed while casually slathering butter on her second ear of corn. "I am. The man is a quintessential narcissist. With a sprinkle of sociopathy on top."

Charlotte's head slowly tilted. "You know what, Ella? You may be onto something. I always suspected he could be behind the threats against me. But the murders? I didn't go that far."

"Why would you? In your mind, he's Corporal Kincaid, here to serve and protect. You'd never think to entertain the idea of him being a criminal."

"Wait, I'm still trying to digest all this," Miles said.

"You two actually believe that Walter could be the Numeric Serial Killer?"

"Yes," they shot back in unison.

"Wow. Well, maybe we need to take another look at that Rush Street surveillance footage from the night Stephen went missing. See if Walter shows up on any of it. Since he said that area is his stomping ground, he may have been out there that night."

"Forget all that," Ella said. "Just go and arrest him now!"

"I wish we could," Charlotte said. "I'd lock him up in a heartbeat."

Ella's cell phone rang. "Oh, no," she moaned.

"What's wrong?"

"That's Elijah texting me. I told him I'd be back in River Valley today. We made plans to go out for drinks tonight, but I was so excited about coming to see you that I totally forgot about them."

"Aw, does that mean you have to leave?"

"I probably should. I've got to wash my hair, touch up my manicure, redo my makeup, the whole nine."

"Well, it was so good seeing you," Charlotte said. "Next time, it has to be longer."

"It will. I promise."

Miles followed the sisters out to Ella's car, watching as they clung to one another. He thought about his siblings, Lena and Jake, and realized just how much he missed being with them in Clemmington.

Ella threw her arms around him. "It was so nice meeting you, Miles. Thank you for being here and taking care of my big sis."

"I'm happy to do so. Thank you for coming by and surprising her on such short notice."

After Ella climbed inside her electric-blue jeep and drove off, Miles and Charlotte walked back inside the house arm in arm.

"Should we finish off that delicious bottle of pinot grigio?" she asked.

"Absolutely," Miles murmured, leading her to the deck.

CHARLOTTE'S PHONE PINGED.

"Chief Mitchell is texting me. Maybe he's got a case update."

"Let's hope so," Miles replied, looking over her shoulder.

The pair were curled up on her cream suede sofa in the family room, listening to John Coltrane's *A Love Supreme* album while finishing up a second bottle of wine.

"Ooh, *yes!*" Charlotte squealed. "The chief just received an email from Freelain & Associates. The attorneys are going to bring Stephen's friends in for questioning. I've gotta reach out to them and schedule dates and times."

"Good job." Miles gave her a high five. Their fingers intertwined. She leaned in and kissed his cheek.

The unexpected move stiffened his body. He quickly recovered, loosening his back so not to appear as thrilled as he felt.

"See?" he said. "What did I tell you? I knew we would still get a sit-down with those guys even though they lawyered up."

"Yes, you did. And I appreciate you reassuring me.

Because I was about to lose it." Charlotte set her phone on the coffee table and reclined back on the couch. "This day really took a turn for the better. Thanks to you. I know I say this all the time, but I appreciate you being here, Miles. So much. I don't know if I could've continued working this investigation without you."

"Of course you could have. But like I always tell you, I'm happy to be a part of it. And even happier to have reconnected with you."

Just as Charlotte nestled her head against his chest, her phone pinged again.

"That's probably the chief replying to my message." She examined the screen. "Hmm, this isn't him. It's a text from an unknown number."

"What does it say?"

Charlotte didn't respond. A long line creased her frowning forehead.

"What's wrong?" Miles asked her.

She handed him the phone.

FYI, you got lucky escaping that car chase. Next time I'll succeed in running you off the road, kidnapping you and torturing you for twelve days straight. I'll carve a #12 into your cheek, then leave your perfectly preserved body on the shores of the Creosote River. Your days are numbered, Sergeant Bowman...

Charlotte nestled against him, as if needing to feel protected. "What are the chances of you staying here with me permanently? Or at least until we catch the killer?"

"You already know the answer to that."

Chapter Nine

Charlotte tapped her pen against a notebook and stared across the desk at Stephen's friend Josh. His icy blue eyes appeared puffy and dull, as if he'd been crying. There was a glint of defiance, indicating he didn't want to be there.

A miniature fan propped on the corner of her cluttered desk did little to cool the stuffy office. A pipe had burst in the interrogation room early that morning, forcing Charlotte to question Josh in her small space. Despite stacking plastic bins filled with evidence and research files in a corner, it was still overcrowded. The area wasn't equipped to house five people. But she wanted Miles and Chief Mitchell there as she faced off with Josh and his attorney.

Charlotte spun her laptop around and pointed at the screen. "Is this you in the video?" she asked Josh.

He brushed his floppy blond curls away from his face, his eyelids jumping uncontrollably. "Is that Eden's Den?"

"Yes, it is."

"Then, yeah, that's me."

"So you, Stephen, Hunter and Rob were together when you arrived at the bar. Is that correct?"

"Uh, lemme think. Umm…"

Josh ran his hands down his sunburned arms. He looked like a surfer ready to catch a few waves in his white tank top, palm leaf Bermuda shorts and flip-flops. Charlotte was surprised that his attorney hadn't asked him to dress more appropriately. But she shouldn't have been, considering he was the son of a real estate mogul who owned half of River Valley. The trust fund crowd tended to do whatever they wanted.

"So when we got to Eden's Den," Josh said, "yeah, Stephen was with us. I went to talk to the bouncer, Darryl, because I know him. He works security at one of my dad's shopping centers. He told us we could jump the line, and we did."

"*Who* did?" Miles interjected.

"*Meee*," Josh drawled while counting on his fingers, "Hunter, Rob and…"

He paused for several seconds.

"And?" Charlotte asked.

Josh fidgeted with his grubby fingernails. "I don't know, man. When we got inside the place, it was packed. I mean, wall to wall. And *full* of smoke. We could barely, like, see a thing. So we just went straight to the bar and grabbed some shots or whatever. We downed those and lost each other in the crowd. To be honest with you, I don't even remember how I got home that night."

"Hold on, son," Chief Mitchell said, his right brow lifting. "Back up. Does that mean you don't remember whether or not Stephen ever entered the bar?"

"Yeah. I really don't, sir."

"Oh, boy…" the chief growled, pulling off his glasses and rubbing his eyes.

Charlotte slid her open hand toward the middle of the desk. "Is it okay if we take a look at your phone?"

"Why do you need to see his phone?" Josh's attorney asked.

"Just in case there's something on it that could lead to some answers. Info Josh may have missed because it didn't seem important."

"There isn't," Josh shot back.

"Let us be the judge of that," Charlotte retorted. "We're the experts here. Stephen may have mentioned something in a text message that could allude to where he ended up, or even left a voice-mail message that contains vital information."

Josh sat straight up and pounded his fist against the desk. "I am not a suspect here! I shouldn't have to turn over anything to you—"

His attorney placed his hand on Josh's shoulder, quieting him down. "Would it be possible for you to collect whatever information you need from Stephen's phone, Sergeant Bowman?"

"Stephen's phone was never recovered, Mr. Brown."

He turned to Josh. "I thought Corporal Kincaid told you that Stephen's cell was in police custody."

"Who the hell is Corporal Kincaid?" Josh asked.

"Corporal *Walter* Kincaid."

Miles and Charlotte shot one another curious glances. She studied Josh, who was staring off into space with his mouth hanging open.

Mr. Brown appeared flustered as he ran his hand

across his chubby bearded face. "Josh, you mentioned being softball teammates with Corporal Kincaid, who's with the River Valley PD. Do you not remember telling me that?"

"Ohh!" he yelled. "You mean Big Walt? Yeah! Hell yeah. I know who you're talking about now. That's my boy. He's the Savage Sliders' left fielder. He likes to come out and party with us, too."

A tense silence circulated through the office. Chief Mitchell's pale complexion turned a deep shade of burgundy as he clawed at his forearms. Charlotte slid open her drawer and discreetly handed him a new bottle of oat serum. "Thanks," he muttered, slathering it on while nodding at Josh. "Was Corporal Kincaid out with you the night that Stephen went missing?"

"Lemme think, lemme think…umm… You know, I don't remember. He may have been. But listen, dude. I was drunk. I mean *drunk* drunk—"

"Josh," his attorney interrupted. "They don't need all that detail…"

"I would appreciate it if you addressed me as Chief Mitchell. Not *dude.*"

Josh tugged at the hem of his shorts. "Sorry…"

"Back to your cell phone," Charlotte said. "We aren't interested in any of your personal information. We won't search through your photos or contacts, nothing like that. We're only interested in information that could assist in finding out what happened to Stephen."

Josh turned to his attorney. "Do I have to do this? *I have nudes on my phone,*" he whispered loud enough for everyone to hear.

"You're not going to look at photos or anything unrelated to the case, correct?" Mr. Brown asked law enforcement.

"That is correct," Charlotte replied.

"Wait," Josh pressed, "don't they need an eviction notice to confiscate my cell?"

The attorney placed his hand on Josh's shoulder. "You mean a search warrant. And no, not if you give them the phone voluntarily. If you don't, they'll obtain a warrant and take the phone anyway."

Josh stared straight ahead, silently rocking back and forth in his chair. Mr. Brown leaned toward him and whispered, "They just want to take a look at the last communication you had with Stephen before he was met with foul play. Since you don't have anything to hide, I'd advise you to go ahead and hand over the phone in good faith." He looked at Charlotte and continued, "They won't use anything on that phone to incriminate you."

Several moments passed before Josh pulled the cell from his pocket and tossed it onto the desk. "Fine. Here. Take the damn phone. Just don't look at my nudes. And if you can't resist, *please* don't share them with anybody. My mom would kill me if she knew I was sending naked pictures to my friends."

"Trust me," Charlotte said, "we won't be the least bit tempted."

She called the digital forensics investigator in to take the phone and download the data while Miles pushed the interrogation forward.

"Josh, is there anything else you can tell us about the night that Stephen disappeared? Do you remember encountering anyone strange? Someone who may have followed you guys from The Bottomless Bar to Eden's Den?"

"Not really, no. Looking back, I wish I hadn't gotten so wasted. I would've been more alert. Better able to look out for my boy, you know?"

It was the most sensible thing Josh had said all afternoon.

"I do know," Miles said. "But don't blame yourself. Just do all you can to help us with the investigation."

"I'm trying. I'm trying…"

Charlotte observed Josh as his left leg bounced rapidly. He tugged at his earlobe, mouthing words but not saying anything.

"What's on your mind?" she asked him. "Is there something you're not telling us?"

Josh shrugged and slid forward, resting his elbows against his knees. "Something hit me about that night. But it's probably not important, so…never mind."

"Anything you can tell us about that night is important," Miles said. "So go on. We're listening."

"I remember Stephen stumbling around pretty bad. I mean, *really* bad, after we left The Bottomless Bar. And don't get me wrong. We were all messed up. But Stephen was way worse than the rest of us, even though he drank the least. It got me to thinking. What if somebody roofied him? Do you think that could be a possibility?"

"It certainly could," Charlotte replied just as she noticed Walter loitering near her office.

Please do not try and come in here…

Chief Mitchell seemed to notice him, too. When Walter peeked through the window, the chief stood and headed for the door. "Sergeant Bowman, Detective Love, I'll let you two wrap this up. I need to have a quick chat with someone."

Get him! Charlotte wanted to shout. But instead, she responded, "Thank you, sir. We'll circle back with you once we're done."

"Sounds good. Mr. Tillman, Mr. Brown, thank you for coming in today. We really appreciate it."

Josh hopped up from his chair and saluted Chief Mitchell. "Nice meeting you, Admiral Michaels. Thank you for your service here today."

The chief ignored him and walked out into the hallway. "Corporal Kincaid! In my office. I need to talk to you. *Now.*"

"Do you two have any further questions for my client?" Mr. Brown asked.

"If Josh can't think of anything else that would be helpful," Charlotte said, "then I think that's it. Forensics should be done with the cell phone data download. We'll return it to you on the way out."

"So that's it?" Josh asked, holding his hands up over his head. "You're not gonna arrest me?"

"Do we have reason to?" Miles asked.

Mr. Brown gripped Josh's arm and pulled him out of the chair. "Son, let's go. I pray your father doesn't ask to see a copy of this interrogation video."

Charlotte led them toward the front of the station, her legs heavy with disappointment.

Back to the drawing board, she thought as Josh didn't appear to be their killer.

Chapter Ten

"These dinners of ours keep getting better and better," Charlotte said to Miles from across her dining room table. "But you have to keep your promise. No talk of the investigation."

He glanced down at his plate. "With this helping of sautéed scallops, Parmesan pasta and grilled asparagus you cooked? Trust me. I won't be doing much talking at all."

"Now, that would defeat the purpose of me preparing this special meal for you. This is supposed to be a thank-you, a night off and a chance for us to catch up on things *outside* of work."

"I'm only kidding with you," Miles said, opening a bottle of Ribolla Gialla.

He filled Charlotte's glass and handed it to her. Their fingers brushed lightly against one another's. She shifted in her seat, adjusting the deep sweetheart neckline on her fitted magenta dress.

"Hey, can I ask you a personal question?" he said.

"Sure. Ask away."

"Why did you and your ex-husband split up?"

Charlotte froze mid-swallow. She coughed, a piece of scallop catching in her throat.

"Wow," she said after several sips of wine. "I didn't see that one coming."

"I'm sorry. Are you okay?"

She nodded but didn't proceed in answering the question.

"When you and I first met at that conference," Miles said, "you refused to discuss your divorce. I assumed it must've been pretty intense. I mean, it drove you to use me for my body all weekend long, then kick me to the curb as soon as the last session ended."

"Will you stop it with all the dramatics!" Charlotte insisted, grabbing a dinner roll and pretending to aim it at his head. "If I recall correctly, you had a pretty good time that weekend, regardless of what I would or wouldn't share with you."

"Damn right I did."

His sexy lips pulled into a half smile. Charlotte resisted the urge to swipe everything off the table and pull him on top of it.

"That's why I was so disappointed when you ended things," Miles continued right before his smile faded.

Charlotte took a long sip of wine, then exhaled slowly.

Time to open up. He deserves to know...

"So, I was married to an attorney. A very slick criminal defense attorney whose practice was based in Las Vegas."

"Oh, boy. I can already see where this is going."

"Yeah, and you'd probably be right about everything you're assuming. My ex and I were basically in a long-distance relationship. He spent most of his time in Vegas while I was here in River Valley. Eventually he bought a condo there, and his trips home became less and less frequent. Unfortunately, he fell into all the stereotypical Sin City trappings. High-stakes gambling, escort services, heavy drinking, recreational drugs…"

Miles reached across the table and took Charlotte's hand in his. "I am so sorry you had to deal with that. I figured whatever happened must've been rough. But damn. I didn't expect it to be that bad."

"Thank you, Miles. Believe it or not, things got worse. I found out he and a couple of judges were taking bribes to help their clients get lighter sentences or skip jail time altogether. There were also rumors that he'd gotten caught up with the mob. After I heard all that, I just cut ties, started seeing a therapist and worked to move on."

"Good for you. That couldn't have been easy. And after hearing it, I can understand why you didn't want to share your story. We barely knew one another."

"Plus, it was still fresh when you and I met. I wasn't ready."

"Yet you found it in you to date a clown like Walter, huh," Miles quipped.

"Look, you are not allowed to judge the decisions made by a brokenhearted woman. After that divorce, I was not in my right mind. And in all honesty, my divorce is the reason why I made the mistake of dating Walter. He knew I was vulnerable and took advantage of it."

"What even attracted you to him? He's such a jerk."

Charlotte could hear the pain in Miles's strained tone. She knew he was wondering why she hadn't reached out to him. Charlotte was too embarrassed to tell him that she hadn't been ready for real love back then. She knew deep down that Walter was just something to do. Someone to keep her mind off her ex. At that time in her life, that was all she could handle.

"I don't know," she replied quietly. "But trust me, if I could turn back the hands of time and do things differently, I would."

"So looking back, you have regrets?"

Charlotte looked Miles directly in the eyes. "I do."

She swirled a cluster of noodles onto her fork and nibbled at them. The conversation had managed to disrupt her appetite. The pair remained silent for several moments before Miles finally spoke up.

"I can understand how you felt."

"You can?"

"In a way. I mean, I've never been married obviously, so I can only relate to your experience to a certain extent. But you were in survival mode. And Walter was like low-hanging fruit. He was right there. In your face, every day. Probably sweating the hell out of you to date him."

"That he was."

"What man in his right mind wouldn't be?"

"That was an awfully nice thing for you to say. Thank you. But can we please change the subject? As a matter of fact, how about we turn this conversation around and focus on *your* dating history."

"Oh, no…"

"Oh, no, nothing," Charlotte shot back. "Come on. Spill the beans. Tell me why you're single, and what went wrong in your last relationship."

Miles let out a low moan, stalling as he piled more pasta onto his plate. "I despise the hot seat."

"Well, you made me sit in it long enough, so now it's your turn. And I'm sure your story isn't worse than mine."

"You're right. It isn't. But it's similar. Because in the end, I did get my heart broken."

Charlotte's stomach dropped at the pain on his fallen expression. "I'm sorry, Miles. Listen, you don't have to talk about it if you don't want to."

"No, no. I'm good. I forced your story out of you. It's only fair that I share mine. Bottom line? She cheated."

He shoved a piece of asparagus inside his mouth as if he were done talking.

"Wait, that's it?" she asked. "You're not gonna share any details with me?"

"Do I have to?"

"Of course you do! I just poured my heart out to you. You're obligated to spill every drop of your tea."

"All right. Fine. I just… I can't stand rehashing the situation. But anyway, on one of my visits to LA to visit my sister back when she still lived there, I met a bartender who worked at a spot near the police station."

"Ooh, a bartender. I bet she was pretty, wasn't she?"

Miles shrugged. "She was attractive. As you can imagine, dating someone who works in that industry is tough. She got hit on constantly. Ballplayers, actors, musicians… I was surprised she was even interested in me. I was just a cop."

"So she hit on you first?"

"She did. I figure she was tired of dating industry

men. But in the end, turns out she was just like many of them."

"What do you mean?"

"Well, she got so drunk one night that she forgot I was driving in the next morning to see her. When I got to her place, I was knocking on the door, but there was no answer. I realized the door wasn't closed all the way, so I went inside. Called out her name. Didn't get a response. Walked into the bedroom, and *boom*. Caught her in bed with another man."

Charlotte's mouthful of wine went down so hard that it burned her throat. "*What?* That must've been a horrible experience."

"It was. After that happened, I found solace in serial dating. Took me a minute to realize that I'm a one-woman man. So, I've committed to remaining single until I meet the right person."

The statement lingered in the air. Charlotte remained silent, unable to take her eyes off him.

In that moment, she realized that something had changed within her. Charlotte was having a hard time controlling her attraction toward Miles. Maybe it was everything he'd poured into her investigation. Or that he was still just as fine as he'd been the day they met. The fire between them had never died. They'd simply quelled it for the sake of the case.

"Listen," Miles said, taking their plates. "Enough sad talk about cheating and breakups and therapy. Didn't I see a salted caramel cheesecake from Beatrice's Bakery around here somewhere?"

Charlotte followed him into the kitchen. "You sure did. It's right there on the counter."

"But wait, you didn't clean your plate, young lady. I don't know if you're allowed to have dessert."

"I can't just have a tiny little piece?" Charlotte asked, her silky tone laced with flirtation. She blamed it on the alcohol and kept going. "I thought you were dying to give me a taste.

Okay, too far. Rewind...

"Wait, wait," she stammered. "That didn't come out right."

"It came out exactly how it was supposed to. Because you're right. I am dying to give you a taste."

Miles opened the box of cheesecake, dipped his finger in a dollop of whipped cream and licked it off.

"Don't do that," Charlotte murmured, every nerve in her body buzzing.

"Don't do what?" he asked, repeating the gesture.

"That."

He slid a fork into the cake and held it to Charlotte's mouth. When her lips parted, he slipped it inside.

"Oops," Miles whispered. "I got a bit of graham cracker crust right here in the corner of your..."

He leaned in and kissed her. Charlotte sucked in a breath of air. Her mind told her to take a step back. But her heart told her to stay put. Her heart won.

She melted into the kiss, their lips in perfect sync. Her hands clutched the back of his neck as his held her waist, leading her out of the kitchen.

They stumbled up the stairs, his mouth moving to her ear, then down to her neck. When they reached the bedroom, he paused, staring at her intently as if asking for permission to enter. She responded by pushing him inside, unbuttoning his shirt on the way to the bed.

Chapter Eleven

Miles awakened to the feel of Charlotte's smooth back pressed against his chest. She was still wrapped in his arms, her shoulders moving to the rhythm of her deep breathing.

A satisfied smile lingered on his lips despite the dull pain throbbing over his right eye. It may have been the lack of sleep. Or too many glasses of wine. Either way, he didn't dare get up to search for a bottle of aspirin. He'd dreamed of being back in this position for so long and refused to disrupt the moment.

Charlotte stirred slightly. Miles kissed the back of her neck, hoping she'd awaken for another round of spontaneous lovemaking. But her fluttering eyelids remained closed.

He glanced at the clock. It was almost 6:00 a.m. The alarm was set to go off in thirty minutes. Miles tightened his grip, her body aligning perfectly alongside his. Sleep or awake, he'd relish their last minutes together until it was time to head to the station.

Miles had lain awake most of the night. Being with Charlotte incited an adrenaline rush he couldn't suppress. But their explosive evening wasn't the only cause of his insomnia. While they'd promised to bury all talk of the investigation, their avoidance didn't negate the fact that the clock was ticking and they still had a case to solve. One that might be linked to the threats she herself had been receiving.

A cell phone screen lit up from the mirrored nightstand. Miles raised his head, eyeing its pale pink case. It was Charlotte's.

The buzzing didn't disturb her. He ignored it, resting his face against her hair as he lay back down.

He inhaled the sweet scent of coconut serum. Just as he sprinkled her shoulder with tender kisses, her phone lit up again. And again.

Miles popped up and gently shook Charlotte's shoulder. "Hey, your phone is blowing up. Maybe you should check it. See what's going on."

"Ugh," she groaned, gripping her temples. "My head is pounding. How much did I drink last night? Wait, what even happened last night?"

"You really don't remember?" he breathed, his lips nuzzling her ear.

"Ooh," she sighed sexily, reaching for the phone. "It's all coming back to me now."

He continued running his lips lightly across her shoulder as she checked her cell.

"Oh *no!*" Charlotte hopped up, knocking Miles in the mouth with her elbow.

"*Ow!* What's wrong?"

"Chief Mitchell has been trying to reach me for over two hours! Another body was found. This time at Angler Canyon Reservoir. Female victim. We need to hurry up and get to the crime scene! *Damn*, I hope they haven't transported the body to the medical examiner's office yet," she swore before storming into the bathroom and slamming the door.

Miles rolled out of bed and slipped into his boxers. "I'll meet you downstairs in fifteen minutes!" he called out.

She didn't respond.

This wasn't the way he'd hoped to start their morning.

MILES PULLED INTO the Eagle County Medical Examiner's parking lot. "This is the part I hate most about our job."

"Which part?" Charlotte asked. "Finding out we've got another murder on our hands? Or having to examine the body with the coroner?"

"Both."

The pair had just left Angler Canyon Reservoir. Their victim was identified as Nalah Coldon, a twenty-nine-year-old woman last seen over two weeks ago leaving a bar in downtown River Valley.

"So Nalah definitely fits the description of our killer's other victims," Charlotte said as they entered the gray cement two-story building. "Young, fit, attractive and successful."

"Correct. And she disappeared during a night out with friends, just like everyone else who's turned up dead."

Miles could see the veins protruding from Charlotte's neck. The stress of the case had already kicked back in. She'd been strictly business ever since they left her house earlier that morning, as if their night together never happened.

What do you expect? She's got another homicide to contend with, Miles told himself. Nevertheless, the reminder didn't kill the sting of rejection burning inside his chest.

"Our victim had just made partner at her law firm before she was killed," Charlotte said. "I can't imagine what that poor woman went through in the days leading up to her death."

"Or all of the victims for that matter. It'll be interesting to hear what the medical examiner knows so far."

Charlotte flashed her badge at the receptionist before leading Miles down a long, sterile hallway and onto a set of elevators. A blast of freezing air hit them when the doors opened onto the lower level.

The temperature failed to mask the putrid scent of decomposition. A rush of nausea rumbled inside Miles's stomach. He covered his nose and mouth. But the foul odor still managed to seep through his fingers.

"I'll ask the coroner for masks once we get to his office," Charlotte told him.

He nodded, keeping his mouth tightly closed. She led them through a heavy metal door past a wall of mortuary chambers and into the autopsy suite.

"Hello, Dr. Peterson," Charlotte said.

"Sergeant Bowman. Good to see you."

The medical examiner stood behind a steel table covered with a white body bag. Miles was able to get a better look at him now than he had at Stephen's chaotic crime scene. Dr. Peterson couldn't have been more than five feet tall. Wiry white hair protruded like small bushes from a blue skullcap, while a potbelly poked out from underneath his surgical gown. Droopy jowls, close-set hazel eyes and a toothy grin made him appear more like a comedic actor than a pathologist.

The examiner pointed toward a small wooden closet. "You know where to find the gowns, gloves and masks." He acknowledged Miles with a head nod. "Detective Love, correct? We met out at the Hoptree River, during the recovery of Stephen Seymour's body."

"Yes, we did. Good to see you again, Doctor. Though I wish it were under more pleasant circumstances."

"Most definitely." His eyes lowered as he unzipped the bag. "I'm really hoping you can assist River Valley PD in finally catching the killer, like you did back in California. This is getting to be a real problem that our police department can't seem to handle on their own."

"We're all working hard to make an arrest, sir."

Miles reached over and gave Charlotte's arm a reassuring squeeze. Her muscles tensed underneath his touch. He could tell by her drawn expression that she hadn't taken kindly to Dr. Peterson's statement.

The pair pulled on their protective gear and approached the body.

"This definitely looks like the work of our killer." Charlotte said.

Dr. Peterson nodded, pointing to the victim's left cheek. "I'd say so. Especially considering she's got the number eight carved here."

The scent of rotten eggs drifted from the victim's body. Her skin had already turned a pale shade of gray. Dried blood resembling streaks of rust stained the left side of her face, neck and collarbone.

"Are you suspecting another poisoning?" Miles asked.

"I am. I already drew specimens and sent them off to the forensics lab. The toxicologist promised to put a rush on testing. Maybe we'll luck out this time and something will be revealed in the results."

"Wait," Charlotte said, pointing at the victim's neck. "What about the bruising along her throat? This is the first time I've seen that type of scarring on one of the bodies. Could the cause of death be asphyxiation this time?"

"I don't believe so," Dr. Peterson replied, running his fingertip along her neckline. "The bruising is fairly light. There was no bleeding around the throat, and the hyoid bone at the base of her tongue isn't fractured."

"Were there any splotches in her eyes or on her lungs?" Miles asked.

"No. Nor was her heart enlarged. Further proof that asphyxiation probably wasn't the cause of death. But these are just my initial findings. Once I perform the full autopsy, I'll know more."

Charlotte slowly studied the body from head to toe. "I really hope that the toxicology report comes back positive this time. We need a win in this case. Desperately."

"It's coming," Miles said, wanting nothing more than to reassure her after sensing dejection in every word she spoke.

"Thank you, Dr. Peterson," Charlotte said. "Please contact me with any updates."

"I certainly will."

She ripped off her protective gear and was out of the

autopsy suite within seconds. Miles rushed to keep up with her. Charlotte didn't utter a word as she walked two steps ahead of him all the way to the parking lot.

"Hey, are you okay?" he panted.

"I'm fine."

"Look, I know it seems like this investigation is going from bad to worse. But you're doing everything that you can to solve it."

Charlotte's black pumps screeched along the asphalt as she stopped in the middle of the lot. "Am I? Because last time I checked, I was laid up in bed sound asleep this morning while the rest of River Valley PD was at *my* crime scene. Then when I got there, Walter had taken the lead on the investigation, and Chief Mitchell was asking where the hell I'd been for the past two-plus hours! Do you know how humiliating that was? It was as if he knew you and I were together last night. Meaning, *together* together."

"Listen, Charlotte. You're overthinking this. There's no way the chief would know that. Not to mention, you're human. I'm sure you didn't even realize you'd turned off your ringer."

"False. I did realize it. Because I turned it off on purpose."

"Why would you do that?"

"Because for the first time in a long time, I just wanted to enjoy a night off with some good food, good wine and good company."

Her words pulled him in closer. "And I get that," he said softly, placing his hands on her shoulders. "Everybody's entitled to a break. It's normal. And healthy."

Charlotte pulled away. "Not when you're pursuing a

serial killer. In my case? It was nothing short of stupid."
She paused, shaking her head while looking straight
through him. "I'm sorry, Miles, but I don't think we
should—"

"Please," he interrupted, backing away. "I already
know where this conversation is going. You don't have
to say it."

Her head fell. "I didn't mean to lead you on. I didn't
even expect for things to go as far as they did last night.
But I've got to stay focused. No distractions."

"Understood," he told her, his voice straining against
the knot stuck in his throat. He wanted to address the
whole distraction statement, but at this point, he didn't
have the energy. Or the emotional bandwidth.

Fool me twice, shame on me...

"Where to now?" Miles asked. "Angler Canyon Reservoir?"

"Yes—"

Charlotte stopped at the sound of her buzzing cell
phone. She scanned the screen, cringing at the message.
"Scratch that. Chief Mitchell just texted me. He wants
to meet back at the station. ASAP."

"But what about the crime scene? Shouldn't you be
there processing it?"

She threw open the passenger door and collapsed
into the seat. "Walter is handling it."

Chapter Twelve

"What happened to you this morning?" Chief Mitchell asked Charlotte.

She sat across from him, her jittery knees banging against the edge of his desk.

"Sir, I am so sorry. When I fell asleep last night, my ringer was off, and I didn't hear your call coming in."

"Your *ringer* was off?"

Charlotte picked at her cuticles, wishing she could dissolve into the floor. "Yes, sir."

"Sergeant Bowman, may I remind you that you're investigating one of the deadliest cases this town has ever seen? Your ringer should be on at all times. Is that understood?"

"Absolutely. It was my mistake, and it'll never happen again."

He downed several gulps of piping hot coffee, despite the sweltering temperature inside his office. "What's going on with you, Bowman? Is everything all right?"

"Yes," she insisted, sliding toward the corner of her chair. "Everything is fine. I've been working this case to the bone. Detective Love and I are constantly reviewing the surveillance footage we've collected, con-

stantly poring over the case files, and revisiting the crime scenes over and over again. As a matter of fact, we were leaving the coroner's office and heading back to Angler Canyon right before you called me back here."

"Speaking of Detective Love…"

Charlotte grimaced beneath the scrutiny in his squinting eyes.

"Do you think it's benefiting you having him here? Or has he become more of a distraction than an asset?"

See, I knew it!

Charlotte cleared her throat, choosing her words carefully before speaking them. "Detective Love has definitely been an asset to this investigation, sir. I value his input as well as his skill set. Plus, he's acted as a great sounding board. And I certainly appreciate his protection. I've felt much safer knowing he's got my back, which is a lot more than I can say for some of my colleagues around here. Half of them don't even seem to believe I've been threatened. A couple even have me wondering whether they're behind the threats."

"That's an awfully bold statement to make, Sergeant Bowman."

"Bold, but true."

A stare down ensued as neither of them spoke a word for several moments.

Did I go too far? Charlotte asked herself as the chief's bushy brows arched into his rumpled forehead.

"Sir, may I ask what sparked these questions? Was it the fact that I showed up late to the crime scene this morning? Or is it something else?"

"Well, since you brought up your colleagues in the department, I will share this with you. Some of them think that this case is too complicated for you to handle. Arriving late to the crime scene today, appearing flustered and disheveled, only fueled their argument. You're a sergeant now, and as you know, to whom much is given, much is expected."

"Chief, rest assured that I *can* handle this case. I am confident that this latest victim is going to lead us to the killer. While we were at the medical examiner's office, I took a close look at Nalah Coldon's body. Her murder appears a bit different than the others, starting with the fact that she has some bruising around the neck. Maybe our suspect is slipping. I have yet to fully process the crime scene myself. Once I do that, question the victim's friends, and receive the full autopsy and toxicology reports, I will have some definitive answers."

Chief Mitchell grabbed a pile of papers sliding off his desk and stacked them neatly. "I believe in you, Bowman. And I do trust that you'll solve this case. That's why you were promoted to sergeant and assigned to it over everybody else in the department—"

He was interrupted when Walter came bursting into the office, panting like a rabid dog.

"Chief!" he yelled. "Sorry for the interruption, but I need to speak with you. Immediately."

Charlotte leapt from her chair. "*Excuse* me, Corporal Kincaid. Chief Mitchell and I are in the middle of a meeting."

He grinned arrogantly. "That's why I pardoned myself first. Plus, it's good that you're here. I was planning on sharing this with you, too." He shoved his hands inside his pockets and sauntered toward the desk. "Sir, I found a syringe near the crime scene."

"You *what*?" Charlotte uttered.

"*I* found a syringe near the crime scene," Walter repeated, much louder this time. "I'll send it off to the lab for testing this afternoon."

While Charlotte was happy for the discovery, she wanted to slap the sneer off his smug face.

Chief Mitchell broke out into a slow clap. "Good work, Corporal. That syringe may be the first piece of viable evidence collected at any of the crime scenes."

"I know, right?" Walter jabbed his crooked index finger in Charlotte's direction. "Maybe it wouldn't have been such a bad idea to partner up with me after all."

"How about we wait and see what forensics reports back before you break out the champagne?" she suggested.

"I don't know, Sergeant," Chief Mitchell said. "Corporal Kincaid might be right. Maybe you should rethink teaming up with him on this investigation."

Just as Charlotte opened her mouth to object, Miles appeared in the doorway.

"Sorry to interrupt. Detective Bowman, the manager of The Tipping Point just called. She pulled the surveillance footage from the night Nalah was there."

Charlotte turned to Chief Mitchell. "Sir, are we done here? I need to get back to my investigation."

"You mean *our* investigation?" Walter quipped. He nudged Miles. "Did you hear the news? I found a syringe at the crime scene today. Already sent it off to the lab for testing."

Miles nodded, his poker face in full effect. "Great work, Corporal Kincaid. I hope it leads us straight to the killer."

"*Us?* Don't you mean *me?* Because at this point, I feel like I'm carrying this entire case all by myself."

"You *cannot* be serious," Charlotte spat just as Chief Mitchell rose to his feet.

"Hold on, hold on. Let's reel it in. Sergeant Bowman, I know you're anxious to review that footage from The Tipping Point. Why don't you and Detective Love head there now, then go by Angler Canyon once you're done?"

"Yes, sir—"

"Wait," Walter said, stepping in front of Charlotte as she tried to walk out. "Why don't *I* go to The Tipping Point with Sergeant Bowman since I wanna see the surveillance, too, then escort her to Angler Canyon? After all, I am the one who examined the scene this morning."

Charlotte held her breath, praying Chief Mitchell wouldn't go for it.

"Well..." the chief began right before her phone buzzed. She checked the calendar notification, then smiled.

"Oh, look," she said, shoving the screen in Walter's face. "Your in-service training session on traffic and parking enforcement is scheduled to begin in fifteen minutes. Have you set up the conference room and sent a reminder to the attending officers yet?"

"Dammit," he muttered. "Can't you get somebody else to do it—"

"Oh, *no.* I certainly cannot. As the corporal of River Valley PD, it is your responsibility to conduct those sessions."

Walter pushed past Miles on his way out the door.

"I still wanna review that surveillance footage once you retrieve it!"

"Of course you do!" She snickered at the sight of him storming down the hallway.

"Sergeant Bowman?" the chief said. "Don't let today's hiccup happen again."

"I won't, sir. You have my word."

THE TIPPING POINT was bustling during downtown's happy hour. Patrons spilled out of the nautical-themed bar's heavy wooden door and onto the street.

Before heading there, Miles had insisted he and Charlotte spend some time looking into phone records to see if they could trace any of the threatening calls she'd been receiving. Nothing useful turned up. Whoever was making those calls used an untraceable burner phone.

On the way inside the bar, Miles wrapped his arm securely around Charlotte and led her through the rowdy crowd. They weaved their way around the packed tavern, squeezing between white high-top tables filled with groups of friends and coworkers toasting drinks and gyrating to the beat of techno music.

Colorful mainsails hung from the ceiling, and surfboards lined the walls. Shirtless male servers wore captain's hats and white trunks, while the women sported tank tops and mini wrap skirts.

"This place looks like *The Love Boat* meets *Too Hot to Handle*!" Miles yelled over the music.

"Yeah, it's a lot to take in! I think that's the manager in the back, hanging the anchor on the wall."

"I'll lead the way." Miles's grip on Charlotte's waist

tightened as they made a beeline toward the petite blonde. Last night's memory of his hands gripping her hips flashed through her mind.

Shake it off, she told herself as they approached the manager.

"Hey!" the woman chirped, flipping her bouncy bob over her shoulder. Her bright green eyes and neon white smile appeared innocent, almost angelic. But her muscular biceps and six-pack abs served as a warning that she was far from fragile. "I'm Piper. You're Sergeant Bowman, right?"

"Yes, that's me." Charlotte shook her extended hand.

"I just got a call from your partner," Piper said. "Corporal Kincaid?"

Charlotte and Miles threw one another looks of annoyance.

"Interesting," Charlotte responded. "Was he asking about the surveillance footage you have of Nalah Coldon?"

"He was. He asked if I could email it to him. But our internet is down, so I wasn't able to send it." She reached into the back pocket of her white denim shorts and pulled out a USB flash drive. "I saved the footage on this. Oh, and by the way, the two friends Nalah was with the night she went missing are here now."

"They are?" Miles asked. "Where?"

"Over at the bar. See the redhead with the high ponytail and the girl next to her with the platinum buzz cut? Those are her girls."

"We should go and talk to them," Charlotte suggested to Miles.

Piper pointed across the room toward a faux porthole hanging on the wall. "While you're at it, you might wanna talk to Nalah's ex-boyfriend, too. Unfortunately, he's also here."

"Which one is he?" Charlotte asked.

"The jerk with the short mohawk dressed in the tight orange T-shirt, hanging off those two women who clearly don't wanna be bothered with him. His name is Tommy. He was here the night that Nalah went missing. He harassed her from the minute she walked through the door until the minute she left. You'll see it all on the surveillance video. Watch closely. When Nalah left the bar, he followed her out."

"Did he ever come back in?" Miles asked.

"No. He didn't."

Charlotte shook Piper's hand. "Thank you for that information. If we need anything else, we'll be in touch."

She and Miles headed toward the front. "Who should we tackle first?" Charlotte asked. "The friends or the ex-boyfriend?"

"Definitely the ex. But I don't want the friends to leave before we get a chance to talk to them."

"Good point." Charlotte reached inside her purse and pulled out a couple of business cards. "Why don't you go over to the friends, introduce yourself and give them my card? See what they're willing to share. While you do that, I'll go talk to the ex."

"You got it."

Charlotte watched Miles walk toward the bar. He moved with ease as the crowd parted a path for him. Women's gazes lingered on his handsome face and fit physique. He ignored the attention, focusing on reaching Nalah's friends.

That cool demeanor was what attracted Charlotte to him the moment they'd met, and what drew her into the bedroom the night before. For a brief moment she softened, realizing that she'd been too rough on him. But then Chief Mitchell's words popped into her mind.

Don't let today's hiccup happen again...

The reminder sent Charlotte straight across the bar toward Tommy.

Nalah's ex stood with his shoulders slumped, holding a beer in each hand and swaying his hips in between two women.

"Aw, come on, ladies!" he yelled. "I don't see nothing wrong with a little threesome—"

"For the tenth time," one of the women interrupted, "would you please get the hell away from us?"

Tommy held his finger to her head. "I've got a better idea. How about you suck my—"

"*Excuse* me," Charlotte cut in. "Tommy, I'm Sergeant Bowman with the River Valley PD. I'd like to speak with you regarding your ex-girlfriend, Nalah Coldon. Can we go outside and talk?"

He propped his elbow on the table and eyeballed Charlotte from head to toe. "Mmm...a police sergeant, huh. Sweetheart, you're way too fine to be working in law enforcement."

"Oh, am I?" Charlotte asked, casually opening her dark green blazer and exposing her holstered Glock 22.

"What the..." Tommy flinched, falling back into a stool.

"I would advise you to show some respect, young man," she continued. "Now, do you want to step outside and talk to me? Or should I place you in handcuffs and take you down to the station, where you can be formally interrogated?"

The two women Tommy had been harassing snickered and walked off. His long, gaunt face fell sheepishly. "Can we go out back? I don't want everybody to see me talking to the cops."

"Sure. Show me the way."

Charlotte stopped by the bar and grabbed Miles, and together, they followed Tommy out to a patio that was closed to the public due to construction. He rested against a metal guardrail and crossed his arms, staring down at the ground. "If you're gonna ask whether or not I killed Nalah, the answer is no."

Charlotte pulled her cell phone from her purse, opened the Voice Memos app and hit the record button. "According to video surveillance, you were the last person seen with her before she went missing. Didn't you follow Nalah out of this bar that night?"

"I did. But that's because I was pissed off after she walked away while I was in the middle of a sentence. You can't just disrespect me like that."

"Were you yelling at her and getting physical, too?" Miles probed. "Because according to eyewitnesses, you two were in the middle of a pretty heated argument before she left. And is it true that you tried to restrain her before she was able to get away?"

Tommy chuckled condescendingly. "Sounds like Nalah's girls have been in your ear. I saw you over at the bar gossiping with them."

"Gossiping?" Charlotte said. "That's not what we call it. Detective Love and I are here to gather information in hopes of making an arrest."

"What's up with you, dude?" Tommy asked Miles. "You can't speak for yourself? Gotta have a chick talk on your behalf?"

Charlotte snatched a pair of handcuffs out of her pocket.

"Okay, okay!" Tommy threw his hands in the air. "I'll cool out. Look, I was drunk that night. *Really* drunk. Nalah and I had just broken up. I saw her dancing with some dude, and it set me off. So I confronted her about it. And that…that turned into a big blowup."

"What happened after you followed her out?" Miles asked.

"We stood on the street and fought."

"For how long?"

Tommy shrugged, digging his thumbnail into the gap between his two front teeth. "I don't know. Ten, fifteen minutes?"

"How did the argument end?"

"Nalah had the valet guys pull her car around and left."

"Do you remember which direction she went?"

"East on Silver Street. I assumed she was heading home."

"And where did you go?" Miles asked.

"Back inside the bar. Partied till it closed at three in the morning, then took some chick home with me."

"Hmph, that can easily be proven true or false once we review the surveillance footage," Charlotte told Miles before turning to Tommy. "Wait, what do you mean, *some chick*?"

"I—I'm drawing a blank on her name."

Miles's notepad fell to his side. "Let me get this

straight. You were upset with Nalah for dancing with someone else but spent the night with a stranger whose name you can't recall?"

"You make it sound so…*salacious*. But yeah. That's what happened."

"No judgment. Just making sure we've got the story straight. I'd advise you to try and remember who she is. We'll need to contact her and confirm your alibi."

Tommy pulled at the wooden beads on his bracelets, his confident smirk twisting into a scowl. "I will."

"Here's my contact info," Charlotte said, handing him a card while Miles jotted down Tommy's number. "If you think of anything, call me. Either way, Detective Love and I will definitely be in touch."

Tommy flicked the card along the edge of his palm. "Look, I may be guilty of a lotta asinine crap, but like I said, I didn't kill Nalah."

A cool blast of air blew onto the patio when the door swung open. Several patrons spilled out onto faux grass.

"Hey!" Piper yelled from inside. "You all aren't supposed to be out there!"

Charlotte turned to Miles. "Do you have any more questions for Tommy?"

"I think that's all I've got. For now."

"We'll be in touch," she told him. "And by the way, your behavior inside the bar? The excessive drinking, harassment and whatever we *didn't* see? Cut it out. Next time I won't hesitate to lock you up for disorderly conduct."

"Yes, ma'am."

On the way back to the car, Charlotte kept her Voice

Memos app going. "So what did Nalah's friends have to say about her and Tommy?"

"They backed up everything Piper told us. Neither of them approved of their relationship. He was controlling from the very beginning. Verbally abusive, which eventually turned physical. They'd encouraged Nalah to press charges on numerous occasions, or at least take out a restraining order. For whatever reason, she always refused. But what's interesting is that they don't think he killed her."

Charlotte paused. "We'll see what comes of the surveillance footage. If Tommy's story doesn't check out, let's bring him into the station for questioning and collect his DNA."

Miles nodded. She tried to make eye contact when he opened the passenger door. He turned away, his expression dark. She knew he wanted to talk more about their night. They needed to. She didn't want the situation to spiral into a repeat of what happened after their first fling.

But now wasn't the time. She'd already gotten called out by the chief for losing focus. Charlotte couldn't let it happen again.

Chapter Thirteen

Miles sat alongside Charlotte behind her desk, watching the surveillance footage from The Tipping Point. His eyes darted back and forth between the computer screen and her side profile. It was the same view he'd had the night before while lying next to her. The subtle slant of her eyes, straight edge of her nose, gentle curve of her lips...

You're doing it again!

The detective propped his hand against his face, blocking the view of hers while watching the screen. He was itching to continue the discussion about their night together. But he couldn't. They were both deep in investigation mode. Plus, Charlotte had already made her stance clear. He wondered whether she regretted what happened between them. He'd find out at some point. Just not now.

"Okay, so there's Nalah," she said, pointing at the monitor. "See her sitting at the bar between the two friends?"

"I do. And you can see Tommy in the frame, too. He's at that table about six feet over, slowly inching his way toward her."

"Yep, *aaand* here he comes. He's tapping her on the shoulder. Look at how she waves him off. A clear indication that she didn't want to be bothered."

"Yet he just stands there, continuing to harass her," Miles said.

The pair watched as Tommy grabbed Nalah's waist and twisted her body back and forth.

"So he's just gonna force her to dance with him?" Charlotte asked.

"Looks like it."

Nalah pressed her hands against Tommy's chest. He held on to her as she writhed back and forth, struggling to escape his grip. Her friends jumped in and tried to pull him off. He pushed them away. The redhead fell back against the bar. Nalah went completely still, then slapped Tommy across the face.

"Whoa!" Charlotte exclaimed. "Okay, things are getting intense. This is when the police should've been called. I wonder if Piper saw any of it."

Tommy grabbed Nalah by the shoulders and pulled her out of the frame.

"According to her friends," Miles said, "they were regulars at The Tipping Point, and everyone was used to seeing them fight. It was a normal occurrence. So my guess is that people just turned a blind eye to it."

Nalah reappeared in the frame, approaching her friends as if nothing happened.

"She seems pretty unaffected by Tommy's behavior, too." Charlotte tapped the screen. "Look, now she's talking to some other guy."

"Maybe he's the one Tommy was referring to when

he mentioned getting upset over her dancing with some-one else."

As soon as the words were out of his mouth, Nalah hugged the man. Her hands glided over his broad shoulders, ripped pecs and biceps, which were bulging through a fitted white T-shirt. He brushed her bangs away from her face. The pair began swaying back and forth. Then Tommy reappeared in the frame.

"Uh-oh," Miles uttered. "Here we go."

Tommy stood inches away from the man. Nalah tried to hold him off. He shoved her, prompting the man to grab the straps of Tommy's tank top and knock him back. Tommy fell to the floor.

"Wait," Charlotte said. "Why is Nalah running over to help Tommy?"

Miles's eyes narrowed as he watched her help him up off the floor. She held him back as he tried to confront the man. Her friends shook their heads while backing away.

"Ugh," Charlotte groaned. "I hate to see this. Nalah's girls don't seem to wanna get involved at this point. They're probably used to witnessing this vicious cycle of abuse and are tired of getting in the middle of it."

"Can you blame them? So many women end up hurt or dead trying to defend their friends from abusive partners."

The man who Nalah had been dancing with shook his head before walking off. She didn't seem to notice as her focus remained on Tommy, who was now flapping his hands in her face.

"Oh, look," Charlotte said. "After Nalah helped him get back on his feet, he's going off on her again."

"This is unreal. And to know that it all ends with Nalah turning up dead is chilling. I'm fighting the urge to jump through the screen and warn her. Save her. *Something.*"

"I feel the exact same way."

Tommy grabbed Nalah's arm and pulled her toward the back of the bar. They were out of the frame for a few minutes before returning. He put in her a headlock. She ducked down and managed to wriggle out of it.

"I cannot believe everybody is just standing around watching these two go at it like this without doing anything," Charlotte said.

"Including the bartender. He's back there flirting with women and serving drinks as if nothing's happening. And I know it's nobody's responsibility, but damn. Whatever happened to helping out a fellow citizen?"

"Like we said earlier, maybe they're all just used to it. Not to mention they seem too drunk to care."

Miles rubbed his chin, focusing on Tommy as he wrapped his hand around Nalah's throat. "Judging by the looks of this video, Tommy is way more violent than I'd expected. I'm curious to see if the story he told us about Nalah leaving without him holds up."

No sooner than the words were out of his mouth, he caught a glimpse of Nalah running for the exit.

"Look, she's leaving the bar. And Tommy is following her out. Can you zoom in? We can see what's going on outside through the window."

Charlotte expanded the screen. The valet stand was in clear view. Nalah stormed the attendant, shoving her ticket into his chest. She frantically pointed down the street and pushed the man in that direction. Tommy stood inches away from her with his arms behind his back, talking in her ear.

"He's trying to be discreet now that they're outside," Charlotte said. "But it's obvious he's still harassing Nalah. She's trying to get away from him, but he's holding on to the back of her dress so that she can't move. And look at how she's wincing, pulling her head away from his. She can't escape his grasp."

"This is so hard to watch."

A white convertible pulled in front of the bar. Nalah jerked away from Tommy and ran around to the driver's side. She dug around inside her purse, pulled out several bills and practically threw them at the attendant.

Miles sat straight up, trying not to blink as he studied the screen. Nalah climbed inside the car. Tommy approached the passenger door. Right before she pulled off, he hopped inside.

"Hold on!" Charlotte boomed. "What the hell just happened?"

"Tommy lied to us. That's what happened. It'll be a half-truth if he reappears in this footage, walks back inside the bar, then leaves with some other woman."

"I highly doubt that's gonna happen."

The video lasted another 27 minutes. Nalah's car never reappeared. Neither did Tommy.

Charlotte slammed the laptop shut. "And there you have it. Time to bring Tommy in for questioning and a cheek swab."

Chapter Fourteen

River Valley PD's tiny interrogation room still smelled of fresh paint. Tommy sat on one side of a wobbly wooden table, staring down at his hands while pressing his fingertips together so hard that they trembled. Charlotte was seated across from him, looking on intently with her chin propped against her fist. Miles sat in between them, his black metal chair positioned inches away from Tommy's.

"Thank you," she said to Officer Haney after he collected Tommy's DNA. The second he left the room, she went in.

"So, Tommy, why did you lie to us?"

"I didn't lie. I just… I didn't tell the whole story."

She glanced down at her recorder, making sure the red light was on. "And what was the whole story again?"

He groaned, his lean frame slumping down into the chair. "Me and Nalah got into a huge fight inside the bar. She stormed out during the middle of it. I followed her out because I wasn't done talking. She called for her car, and by the time it arrived, I *still* wasn't done. So I got inside the car with her so I could finish what I was saying."

Loyal Readers
FREE BOOKS Voucher

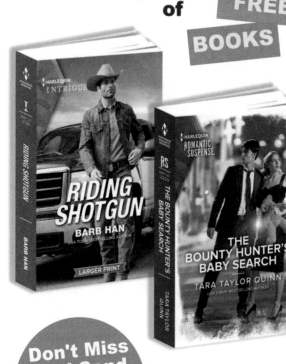

Get up to 4
FREE FABULOUS BOOKS
You Love!

To thank you for being a loyal reader we'd like to send you up to 4 FREE BOOKS, absolutely free when you try the Harlequin Reader Service.

Just write "YES" on the Loyal Reader Voucher and we'll send you 2 free books from each series you choose and a Free Mystery Gift, altogether worth over $20.

Try **Harlequin® Romantic Suspense** and get 2 books featuring heart-racing page-turners with unexpected plot twists and irresistible chemistry that will keep you guessing to the very end.

Try **Harlequin Intrigue® Larger-Print** and get 2 books featuring action-packed stories that will keep you on the edge of your seat. Solve the crime and deliver justice at all costs

Or **TRY BOTH and get 2 books from each series!**

Your free books are completely free, even the shipping! If you continue with your subscription, you can look forward to curated monthly shipments of brand-new books from your selected series, always at a discount off the cover price! Plus you can cancel any time.

So don't miss out, return your Loyal Readers Voucher today to get your Free books.

Pam Powers

LOYAL READER
FREE BOOKS VOUCHER

YES! I Love Reading, please send me up to 4 FREE BOOKS and a Free Mystery Gift from the series I select.

Just write in "YES" on the dotted line below then return this card today and we'll send your free books & gift asap!

➡ — — YES — — ⬅

Which do you prefer?

☐ **Harlequin® Romantic Suspense**
240/340 HDL GRRX

☐ **Harlequin Intrigue® Larger-Print**
199/399 HDL GRRX

☐ **BOTH**
240/340 & 199/399 HDL GRSM

FIRST NAME | LAST NAME

ADDRESS

APT.# | CITY

STATE/PROV. | ZIP/POSTAL CODE

EMAIL ☐ Please check this box if you would like to receive newsletters and promotional emails from Harlequin Enterprises ULC and its affiliates. You can unsubscribe anytime.

HI/HRS-622-LR_MMM22

"And that's a completely different story from what you told Sergeant Bowman and me at The Tipping Point," Miles reiterated. "Which, once again, means you lied."

"Look," Tommy said, slamming his fist into his palm as he spoke, "after Nalah pulled off, she drove around the block a few times while I said my piece. Once I was done, she dropped me back off at the bar."

"We have eyewitness accounts from people who saw you leave the bar with Nalah but never return."

"*Eyewitnesses?* What eyewitnesses? You still talking about Nalah's hatin' ass friends? Or The Tipping Point's manager, Piper? Also known as Piper the Pill Popper. You can't trust a word that woman says. If she isn't drunk, she's high. Or both. Half the time that chick doesn't know whether she's coming or going."

"She seems pretty reliable to me," Charlotte told him. "And sober. Unlike you, she didn't waver on her memory of what took place that night."

Miles spun the laptop around and played the footage of Tommy riding off with Nalah. "Not to mention the surveillance footage doesn't lie. We saw you leave with Nalah, but according to the footage, you never returned."

Silence fell over the room. Charlotte tapped the tip of her pen against the table. Tommy's eyes diverted from her piercing glare to the drab olive carpet.

He's breaking. Keep pressing. The confession is coming...

"You can't even look at me, can you?" she asked.

His bulging pupils slowly rolled back up. He stared directly at her. "Look, Nalah was an attorney. I know how all this works. I didn't even have to come down here and talk to you if I didn't want to. I could've lawyered up. But I didn't. Because I'm innocent."

Miles scooted closer to Tommy and pointed in his face. "Then tell us what the hell really happened that night. What are you hiding from us?"

"Nothing!" A lone tear trickled down his cheek. "Look, I know I ain't right. I know I wasn't a good boyfriend to Nalah. But I didn't kill her. I loved her. I just…"

"You just what?" Charlotte asked, softening her tone at his show of emotion.

"I can't help but blame myself for what happened to her. And that's killing *me*."

"Why do you blame yourself?"

"Because had I not gotten drunk and acted a fool that night, she…she never would've left the bar," Tommy sputtered, choking on his words. "And whoever did this to her never would've gotten ahold of her to begin with, because she would have been with me."

"All right, then," Miles said. "Once again, tell us what really happened. Because if you didn't do it, then Sergeant Bowman and I need to get back out there and investigate who did."

Tommy's chest expanded as he sucked in a breath of air. "The reason I didn't show back up in that surveillance video is because Nalah dropped me off in the back of The Tipping Point. Not in the front."

"By the patio, where we questioned you?" Charlotte asked.

"Yeah, back there. Before I could go inside, this chick stopped me. She was standing outside smoking a blunt.

She was flirting real heavy, asking if I wanted to take a hit. She was cute or whatever. Smokin' hot body. And Nalah had pissed me off. So I took a hit and chilled with her."

"Is this the woman you took home, whose name you can't remember?"

"Yes. Her."

Miles flipped to a blank page in his notebook. "Do you remember her name now?"

"I do. It's Candy."

"Candyyy..." Charlotte said, holding out her hand. "Do you know her last name?"

"Yeah. Cain."

"Cain?"

"Right. Cain."

"The woman's name is *Candy Cain*?" Charlotte repeated.

"Yes. According to her. Now, is that her government name? I don't know. You'd have to ask her."

"Trust me," Miles said, "we will. Have you been in touch with her since Nalah's murder?"

"I have. We're, um…we're kind of dating now."

"In a new relationship already, huh." Charlotte pointed at his cell. "Would you mind passing along her phone number so we can reach out and confirm your alibi?"

"I'll do you one better. I was gonna stop by her job when I left here. Why don't we go there together? You two can talk to her in person and acquit me now or whatever you call it. Declare me innocent, reverse the charges…"

Miles turned to Charlotte. "What do you think?"

"I think that would be great. Keep this investigation moving forward."

"Cool," Tommy said, jumping up from the table. "I'll drive."

"*I'll* drive," Miles shot back, leading them out of the station.

Chapter Fifteen

Miles let up on the accelerator.

"There it is," Tommy said, pointing at a run-down shack on the left side of the road.

"There *what* is?" Charlotte asked.

"Candy's office."

"Office?" Miles snorted. "That looks more like an oversize outhouse to me. Where the hell are we, anyway?"

"Right outside of River Valley," Charlotte told him. "In a town called Gunderson. It's unincorporated, with a population of less than a thousand. And this is no office, obviously. It's a strip club called Razzle Dazzle. Patrons love this place thanks to the inconspicuous location and unassuming exterior. Hence no sign outside."

The parking lot was jam-packed. Miles found a space in the very back and glanced at his watch. "Two fifteen in the afternoon during the middle of the week, and this place is completely full."

"Hey, what can I say," Tommy replied, jumping out and skipping giddily toward the entrance. "The music is good, the buffalo wings are even better, and the dancers? *Whew!* They're the best."

"I'm guessing Candy Cain is a dancer here?" Charlotte asked.

"Candy Cain is the *top* dancer here."

Miles rolled his eyes, following Tommy inside. He almost choked on the streams of smoke billowing through a long, dark hallway.

Tommy approached an overly tanned shirtless man standing near the bar. His bony chest and frail arms were on full display underneath a dusty black leather vest, likening him to an aging rock star.

The man gave Tommy a high five and pointed toward the stage. A dancer dressed in a red-and-white thong was sliding down a pole, swinging her legs to the beat of a bass drum. An array of rowdy men, from suit and tie types to rugged cowboys, stood around the rickety stage, cheering her on while tossing money in the air.

Tommy blew the woman a kiss, then waved frantically at Miles and Charlotte. "Come on!"

The aging rocker tipped his cowboy hat at the pair when they walked by.

"Looks like Tommy's trying to turn this interrogation into a social hour," Charlotte muttered in Miles's ear.

"Yeah, he needs to reel it in. Don't worry. I'll keep him on course."

Multicolor strobe lights swirled overhead, turning Tommy's pale complexion into varying shades of yellow, purple and blue. He pivoted at least three times, staring excitedly around the tiny club before pointing at an empty table. "Do you all wanna grab seats near the stage? Or hang out at the bar until Candy's set is over—"

"We'll wait over by the bar," Miles quickly replied,

diverting his attention away from the scantily clad women scattered everywhere.

Tommy shoved his hand inside his pocket and pulled out a wad of dollar bills. "All right, I'll bring Candy over as soon as she's done."

Two stools sat empty on the far end of the bar. Miles led Charlotte toward them, keeping his eyes fixated on the dingy burgundy carpeting along the way. He could feel her watching him while she giggled softly into her collar.

"What's so funny?" he asked.

"You! It's so cute how stiff and uncomfortable you are. Not much of a strip club guy, huh?"

"Um, *no.* Not at all. The only time you'd catch me in a place like this is if I absolutely had to be there."

"Under what circumstances would you absolutely have to be at a strip club?"

Miles threw his arms out at his sides. "Moments like this! Or if I had to celebrate a friend's bachelor party, or birthday party, or...*whatever.* Some men try and find any reason under the sun to hang out at strip clubs."

"Humph. Well, I'm glad you're not one of them."

Miles almost asked why she'd care either way. It didn't seem as if she wanted anything to do with him beyond business. But he steered clear of the subject.

Get out of your feelings. She's not on that. So you shouldn't be, either. Stay focused on the case...

Tommy came dancing over with Candy by his side.

"Sergeant Bowman, Detective Love, I'd like for you to meet my future wife, Mrs. Candy Cain dash Thompson."

"Nice to meet you both," she purred, extending her hand.

Miles wrapped his fingers around her flimsy grip,

careful not to cut himself on her bloodred acrylic nails. She pulled away quickly without making eye contact.

"Is there somewhere quiet we can talk?" he asked. "Sergeant Bowman and I don't want to take up too much of your time. We just have a couple of questions."

"Not really," she said, running her fingers through her spiky platinum-blonde wig. "And I can tell you right now, Tommy didn't kill that girl. He was with me that night. And *ooh*…what a night it was…"

Miles flinched at the sight of her biting Tommy's cheek.

"Ouch!" Tommy squealed, chomping his teeth toward her neck. "Come on, babe. This is serious. We can get to the good stuff later."

"Sorry, snooks. You're just so irresistible—"

"Look," Charlotte said, "Detective Love and I need your official statement that you and Tommy were together that night, for the *entire* night, in order to clear his name."

"Here it is. My official statement. Thomas Thompson was with me the entire night that the girl went missing. He did not kill her… *Wait!"*

Candy paused, then pulled away from Tommy and punched him in the shoulder.

"Ow!" he howled. "Babe, what was that for?"

"Babe! Don't you have a Ring security system at your house?"

"Yeah. Why?"

"Duh. Because! It should've recorded us going into your house that night your ex disappeared, then leaving the next day."

Tommy broke into a round of applause. "Girl, you are good. I mean, *really* good."

Miles glared at Tommy as he toyed with Candy's peppermint-shaped earring. "You mean to tell me you've had a recording that could prove your whereabouts this whole time and didn't say anything?"

"Dude, I didn't even think about—"

"Detective Love," Charlotte corrected.

"Sorry. *Detective Love,* I've been so caught up in the rapture of Candy Cain that I didn't even think about it."

"Tommy, you do realize that you're a person of interest in Nalah's murder investigation, don't you?" she asked.

He shrugged, focusing on Candy rather than Charlotte. "I guess I just assumed you all would get that I'm innocent."

"Well," Miles began, "that's not how this works. We can't assume anything. If you want to profess your innocence, then we need solid proof. How soon can you get that footage to us?"

"Tonight. I'll grab it the minute I get home." He turned to Candy. "Which will be after my girl gets off work."

"We'll be on the lookout for it," Miles said. "You've got our email addresses. Send it to us ASAP, or else we're going to have another conversation down at the station that won't be as pleasant."

Tommy threw him a salute. "Aye aye, captain!"

Charlotte looked on, shaking her head in disgust. "He really thinks this is a joke."

A commotion erupted near the entrance. Three young men who looked like they'd just stumbled out of a frat house were hurdling over one another, racing toward the stage.

"Why do those guys look so familiar?" Charlotte asked.

Candy rolled her eyes and hid behind Tommy. "Ew. We refer to them as the Rich Boys of River Valley. They throw a lot of money around the club. But they like to get sloppy drunk and way too touchy-feely with the girls."

"Yooo," Tommy breathed, pointing at the group. "Those are Stephen Seymour's boys. That's Hunter in the Gucci joggers, Josh in the long denim cutoffs and Rob in the khakis. They were out with him the night Steph went missing."

"How do you know that?" Miles asked.

"Because I was out that night, too. As a matter of fact, they hit a few of the bars the night Nalah went missing, too." Tommy froze, then rotated back and forth like a robot. "Wait, are you all thinking what I'm thinking?"

"And what would that be?" Charlotte inquired.

"That those guys might be your killers! They were at the exact same spots that Stephen *and* Nalah were the nights they went missing."

"Yeah, and so were you."

Tommy's arms fell by his sides. "Damn. I didn't even think about that…"

The group watched Stephen's crew blow smoke from their mouths as they puffed on cigarettes.

"Hey!" Candy yelled in their direction. "You're not supposed to be smoking in here!"

The aging rocker manning the door held his finger

to his thin, cracked lips, signaling for her to shut up. Candy rolled her eyes and turned away.

"They just let those guys run wild in here. Preppy jackasses. Looking like they stepped straight off the set of *American Psycho*. You all have no idea how twisted they are."

"No, we don't," Miles replied. "How so?"

"They think they can just have their way with anybody. Especially women. Hunter's parents own a vacation home that they use to throw freaky parties and whatnot. I've heard some pretty shady things have gone on out there."

Tommy nudged Candy. "Babe, don't you think you're talking a little too much?"

"No, let her speak," Charlotte said.

"I just don't want my girl getting in too deep. Those guys are trouble."

"You're speaking to the authorities. There is no such thing as getting in too deep. Now, Candy, what types of shady things are you referring to?"

She hesitated, shifting her weight from one silver platform stiletto to the other. "Well… I haven't been to any of the parties personally. But some of the girls from the club have. Those dudes hire them to entertain their friends. They tell them they're just expected to dance, but things usually go way beyond that. Of course, alcohol and drugs are involved. And once a bunch of rich, arrogant douchebags get drunk and high? It's game over."

"What do you mean, game over?" Charlotte asked.

"What I mean is, anything goes. Things get dangerous. Violent, even."

"Okay," Tommy interrupted, wrapping his arm firmly around Candy. "You've said enough. Now you're just speculating. I've been to a couple of Hunter's parties, and they're not that bad. You don't wanna start accusing people of things based on hearsay. Especially dudes like them. They all come from powerful families. Running your mouth can get dangerous. And I don't want those sexy lips of yours getting you into any trouble."

"Where exactly is Hunter's house located?" Miles asked, ignoring his warning.

Tommy tapped his index finger against his chin. "You know, I can't recall…"

"But we can probably find out for—," Candy chimed in just as Tommy broke into a fit of loud coughs. She turned to him, recoiling when his eyes bulged at her.

"Sorry," she muttered. "I don't know where it is."

Pulling a card from her purse, Charlotte threw Candy a knowing look and handed it to her. "If you happen to recall the address, please, give me a call. Tommy, are you sure you don't want to ride back with us?"

"No," Candy answered for him. "He wants to stay here with me."

"You're not wrong," Tommy gushed, nuzzling his nose against hers, then pointing at Miles and Charlotte. "The lady has spoken. I'm staying here."

Miles lobbed a stern head nod in Tommy's direction. "We'll be waiting on that Ring camera footage. Don't make us have to chase you down."

A piercing scream rang out over the music. The group turned toward the stage. Hunter was standing near the edge, tugging at a dancer's leg.

"You know what?" Candy said. "I might remember where that house is after all."

"Babe," Tommy screeched, tightening his grip on her waist. "What do I always tell you? Snitches get stitches!"

She glared at the stage, then at Tommy. "Looks to me like Darlene's the only one who's gonna need stitches. You see the way Hunter's flinging her around that stage!"

"Can-Can," Tommy muttered in her ear, "didn't I tell you to never go against me? Especially in front of company? It's disrespectful."

"Hey, Candy!" the aging rocker yelled from across the bar. "This isn't a rest stop. Your break's over. Get your ass back up on that stage! Big money just walked through the door, and Darlene can't handle them alone."

She pulled away from Tommy and focused on Charlotte, her eyes tearing up. "I'd better go. Sorry I couldn't be more help."

"We appreciate you speaking with us. If you think of anything else you want to share, you have my number."

"Thanks for the ride," Tommy interjected before Candy could say another word. "See ya." He grabbed her hand and pulled her away.

Miles leaned against the bar, watching the pair walk off. "I will never understand why any woman would want to date a man like that. He is a controlling bully. Would barely let Candy speak."

"I agree. But stay tuned. I have a feeling we haven't heard the last of Candy."

Chapter Sixteen

"Are you sure you have to go?" Charlotte asked Miles.

"I wish I didn't. But yes, I do."

Miles rolled his suitcase toward the front door. He'd received a call from his brother that morning with news that a Clemmington cold case was heating back up. Their father asked that Miles get back to town as soon as possible to help sort through the recent developments.

A mix of panic and sadness churned inside Charlotte's stomach as the pair said their goodbyes. She'd gotten used to Miles being there. The thought of him leaving, even if he would only be gone for a few days, wasn't sitting well with her.

"You'll be fine while I'm gone," he said, as if sensing her distress. "Just stick close to home and make good choices. Chief Mitchell is going to make sure you've got extra detail on you. And Officer Haney promised that he'd keep a close eye on you, too. So you're good."

"It still won't be the same. But thanks…"

Miles's cell phone pinged. He checked the notification, then peeked through the blinds. "My car is here. I'd better get to the airport before I miss my flight."

A streak of anxiety shot through Charlotte's rigid

body. Her racing heart implied that this was about more than just Miles's protection. Emotions were taking over. She was having an *absence makes the heart grow fonder* moment before he'd even left.

Shake it off! her inner voice insisted, knowing now was not the time to get emotional. She blinked back the mist in her eyes as he walked out the door.

"I'll be back as soon as I can," he said.

"Good. Don't let your family talk you into abandoning me. At least not before we solve this investigation."

"I won't. The only reason I'm going back is because this cold case means so much to my father."

"What's it about?" Charlotte asked. The question was a combination of curiosity and stalling. She wasn't ready for Miles to leave. They hadn't had a chance to discuss his case since he got the call.

"There's a popular winery located in Clemmington called Vincent Vineyard. The owner and my father were really good friends, until Mr. Vincent turned up dead. He was murdered, and law enforcement never caught his killer."

"Oh, no. I'm so sorry. When did this happen?"

"A little over a year ago. He was stabbed to death at the vineyard, and a knife was recently found buried in the field. So, we're going to question the family again and see what my sister finds after she runs the weapon through forensics."

The car horn blared so loudly that it rattled the bay window.

"Let me get going before this guy leaves," Miles said.

Charlotte grabbed his arm and went in for a kiss on

the cheek. He turned his head before it landed. Their lips ended up connecting.

A moment of stunned silence swirled around them. Miles broke into a curious grin. "Wow. What was that for?"

She shrugged. "I don't know. I guess I'm gonna miss having you around. Even if it is only for a few days. When you do come back, we, uh…we should probably talk more about what happened between us the other night."

"I'd like that."

They embraced for several moments, neither of them wanting to pull away.

"I'll call and let you know when I make it to Clemmington."

"Please do. Safe travels."

Charlotte stood in the doorway, watching as Miles climbed inside the car and pulled off. She stayed there until the vehicle was out of sight.

The buzz of her cell phone pulled Charlotte back inside the house. It almost vibrated off the fireplace mantel before she grabbed it. A text message from an unknown number appeared on the screen.

Stephen's friend Hunter is throwing one of those parties tonight. 8421 Ace Lane. Some of the girls from the club are going. You didn't hear any of this from me. ~ Candy

She paced her living room floor, the soles of her bare feet pounding against the warm wood.

What to do, what to do…

Miles was gone. But there was no way she could miss going to this party. It could lead to finding out more about Stephen's murder. And possibly Nalah's.

She replied to Candy's message.

This will stay between us. Are you planning to attend?

Not sure. Depends on how much Hunter is willing to pay. And whether or not I can sneak away from Tommy. Are you?

I'm not sure either...

While she appreciated the lead, Charlotte didn't want to share her next move with Candy.

She went into her bedroom and slid open the frosted glass closet doors. The brunette bob wig that she'd worn last Halloween was sitting on the top shelf.

"Are you really about to do this?" Charlotte asked herself, knowing that Miles wouldn't approve. Neither would Chief Mitchell. But she couldn't miss out on an opportunity to catch Stephen's friends in action. Plus, if she went in undercover, chances of her being found out were slim to none.

Charlotte pulled the wig down and slipped it over her hair. She turned to the mirror on her bronze vanity table and adjusted the bangs.

"Yep. You're really about to do this."

CHARLOTTE MADE A left turn down Ace Lane. She'd spent the day tracking down dead ends, reaching out to friends of the victims, even ones she'd interviewed before, hoping to find something they'd all missed. Then she'd heard from Miles, who reported he arrived in Clemmington just in time for a major breakthrough on his case, so he hoped to wrap it up ASAP.

The block was dimly lit and fairly calm, with the exception of one house near the corner. She assumed it belonged to Hunter.

She let up on the accelerator, eyeing the luxury cars parked along the curb. The few homes lining the block were lavish, with sprawling lawns and unique, intricately designed architecture.

"In five hundred feet," the navigation system announced, "your destination will be on your right—8421 Ace Lane."

Tires screeched behind her. Charlotte looked in the rearview and saw headlights speeding toward her. The engine roared as a horn blasted. She quickly pulled over just as a neon green Lamborghini sped past.

"Jerk," she muttered.

Charlotte hit the accelerator and drove closer to the party spot. Young women dressed in barely there bikini tops and miniskirts spilled out of the ostentatious wrought iron front door. Shirtless cat-calling men carrying bottles of alcohol chased after them.

"What in the world is going on here…" she uttered, realizing her black maxi dress wouldn't blend in with this crowd.

A cream Rolls-Royce pulled up next to her car. Charlotte froze at the sight of four young men hanging out the window.

"Hey, baby!" one of them yelled. He pointed toward Hunter's house. "You going to the party or what?"

She quickly slipped on a pair of cat-eye sunglasses. "Thinking about it."

"Cool. Meet me out back by the pool for a little drink and a little…you know…" he said with a wink.

Charlotte kept her head down and grabbed her clutch, ready to pull out her Glock if necessary. She waited for the car to pull off before parking and climbing out.

Hunter's contemporary three-level, glass-encased house was surrounded by lush trees and greenery. It was lit up from top to bottom, with gyrating bodies on display in every window. A DJ bopped from side to side in the front of the great room while playing hip hop music that blared through six-foot-tall speakers.

Charlotte walked the perimeter of the property. The infinity edge pool and Jacuzzi out back were packed with topless women and frisky men. Four dancers who she recognized from the Razzle Dazzle stood inside an elaborate white gazebo, passing out drinks to a group of men laid out on gray herringbone wicker club chairs. Charlotte slid her sunglasses down her nose to get a better look. Candy didn't appear to be among them.

"Hunter, *stop!*"

The scream came from the house's second-floor balcony. Hunter was standing dangerously close to the railing, struggling to balance a woman on his shoulders. She gripped his head as he swayed back and forth, clearly intoxicated.

"Put me down!" the woman yelped. "I'm gonna fall!"

"Will you *stop*?" he insisted. "I got you!"

Just as her upper body jolted forward, Hunter's friend Rob swooped in from behind and grabbed her. The woman collapsed into his arms.

"Come on, man, cut it out!" Rob yelled. He clutched Hunter's shoulder and tried to pull him back, but Hunter jerked away.

"I'm coming in hot!" Hunter yelled, climbing up onto the railing.

"Dude! You're gonna kill yourself!"

Before Rob could get him down, Hunter spread his arms out at his sides and jumped off the balcony. Everyone cheered as he flipped through the air and crashed into the pool.

These people are out of their minds...

Charlotte continued through the yard, stopping when two familiar-looking women emerged from the Jacuzzi.

Where do I know them from?

And then it hit her. They were Nalah's friends, the ones she'd been with at The Tipping Point the night she disappeared. Charlotte wondered if Nalah had ever been to one of Hunter's house parties, and just how well the pair knew one another.

She grabbed her phone, eager to tell Miles about the connection between Hunter and Nalah's girls. But then she paused.

I'm not supposed to be here.

The only person who knew Charlotte was attending the party undercover was Cindy, the station's 9-1-1 dispatcher. But she wouldn't understand the significance of Nalah's friends being here.

Charlotte slid her phone inside her purse, then pulled it right back out. "You have got to take photos of all this," she whispered to herself.

She shot several pictures, then slowly pivoted while recording a video of the expansive yard. She stopped on someone who was climbing up an eighty-foot palm tree. It was Stephen's friend Josh.

Out of nowhere, Hunter ran over to the tree and joined him. "Race you to the top!" he called out.

As Charlotte continued taping the shenanigans, a pair of hands slid across her hips.

"Hey, baby," a whiny voice whispered in her ear. "Instead of you standing over here talking to yourself and snapping shots of all the fun, why don't you put that phone away and join in?"

Charlotte jabbed her elbow deep into the person's bony chest and spun around.

"How about you get your hands off me instead?" she asked the short, scrawny kid who looked to be about sixteen. His frizzy red hair flopped in his face when he doubled over in pain. His glasses fell to the ground as he held his stomach.

"Oww," he groaned. "Why'd you do that?"

Charlotte almost felt sorry for him. Almost…

"Because you need to learn some respect, that's why. Maybe then injuries like that won't happen again." She slapped him hard on the back and walked off.

An animalistic howl echoed through the yard. Charlotte cringed while watching Hunter and Josh slide uncontrollably down the palm tree, their bare arms, chests and legs scraping against the bark.

"Somebody help me!" Josh yelled, stopping in the middle of the trunk. "I'm not gonna make it!"

His eyes landed on her. She pulled her bangs farther down her forehead. He tapped Hunter's shoulder, then pointed at her.

"Hey! I think that's the chick who tortured me down at the police station!"

"Where?" Hunter asked, glancing in her direction. "And why the hell would she be at my house? Hey!" he yelled into the crowd. "Somebody bring me a ladder! I've gotta get down from here and bounce five-O up outta my house!"

Within minutes, Rob ran over with a ladder. Charlotte took advantage of the disruption and hurried out of the backyard. She squeezed her clutch, feeling for her Glock. Relief hit knowing it was still there.

Charlotte peered over her shoulder on the way to the front of the house, making sure she wasn't being followed. Between the sunglasses and the wig, she thought she'd disguised herself well enough. Apparently not.

Dread hampered her movement as she shuffled toward the street, her platform wedges dragging along the rutted asphalt.

Just get to the car. Just get to the car...

"Hey!" someone called out. "Wait up!"

Charlotte sped up. But the screech of rubber soles drew nearer. She reached inside her purse, looped her index finger around the gun's trigger, then spun around.

"What do you want?" she screamed.

"Sorry!" someone yelled into the dark space between them.

Charlotte lowered her head, peering over the rim of her glasses. The wimpy redhead she'd encountered by the pool was standing in front of her with his arms outstretched.

"I just wanted to say goodbye. I hope you're not leaving because of me. Maybe I could...get your number?"

The laugh creeping up her throat was stifled when she bit her tongue. "I'm leaving because I need to get home," she said, backing away from him. "And you're way too young for me. I'm sure there are plenty of girls at that party who you could talk to, *if* you're even old enough to be here."

"Roman!" someone yelled from Hunter's front lawn.

"Delilah," the young man talking to Charlotte called out. "I'm in the middle of something here!"

"See!" Charlotte said. "There's one now—" She paused when Hunter and Josh came running to the front of the house. "Oops, gotta go!"

Charlotte hopped inside her car and sped off. The whole way home, she envisioned being hunted down by another vehicle. Her muscles tensed at every red light as she sat there, waiting for a strange car to pull up next to hers. Her eyes darted from the rearview to the side-view mirror. Anxiety rumbled through her stomach. She grew faint at the thought of being attacked again.

"You shouldn't have done this," Charlotte told herself. "You should not have come out here alone, without Miles."

She couldn't shake the feeling that she was being followed. Or watched. When her house appeared up ahead, Charlotte hesitated to pull into the driveway for fear that someone would jump out from behind the bushes and pounce.

The car's bright lights shone along the road, displaying empty sidewalks and front lawns. Neighbors' homes were pitch-black. All was quiet. Charlotte reluctantly crept into her driveway. Her headlights beamed through the shrubbery. No shadowy figures appeared to be lurking in the pink oleander hedges.

She drew her gun and climbed out of the car, hurrying inside of the house without incident.

See, you were just being paranoid...

Charlotte secured the top and bottom locks, kicked off her shoes and headed to the kitchen. After pouring a glass of wine, she set up shop in the living room and scanned the photos she'd taken at the party.

How in the hell am I gonna tell Miles about all this?

She grabbed her laptop and connected the USB cord to her phone. As the photos downloaded onto the computer, she clicked open the case file and added a few notes on the evening's events.

Once she was done, Charlotte double-clicked the folder that contained photos from Nalah's crime scene. She shuffled through the pictures, studying images of the medical examiner standing over Nalah's body, the forensics team placing evidence inside of brown paper bags, and Chief Mitchell, who was busy giving police officers directives.

And then there was Walter. He'd somehow managed to appear in almost every photo.

"No surprise there..."

Charlotte tapped on a picture of Chief Mitchell speaking to someone in the crowd. A man standing near him caught her eye. She zoomed in on the image.

Her glass of wine almost slipped from her hand. Charlotte knew that face. It was Hunter.

"What in the hell was *he* doing there?"

She grabbed her phone, so tempted to call Miles and tell him everything. But it was late. And she didn't want to disrupt him while he focused on his father's investigation.

"Just be patient," she told herself, setting the cell aside and turning her attention back to the computer.

Just when the download was complete, the lights went out.

"Oh, come on!"

Charlotte glanced around the room. The glare from her computer screen created a creepy glow that spanned the vicinity. The entire first floor of her house looked like a scene straight out of a horror movie.

Where was the flashlight? And the fuses? And the fuse *box*?

"Miles chose the wrong time to leave me here alone..."

She stood and turned on her cell phone's flashlight. It barely shone through the darkness. Charlotte pitched it, not wanting to waste the battery that needed recharging, and felt her way toward the kitchen.

On the way there, a dark figure hurried past the living room window. She stopped, holding her breath while staring outside. Another figure rushed by.

Where is my gun?

A hushed commotion stirred outside the front door. Charlotte's head swiveled as she searched the living room for her weapon. It wasn't there.

You left it in the kitchen!

She remained stuck in that same spot, watching the window as voices seeped through the cracks.

"Hey, Linda!" someone yelled from the street. "Are your lights out, too?"

"Yes!" her next-door neighbor hollered back. "Are yours?"

Charlotte tiptoed to the window and peeked through the blinds. Linda, who lived two houses down, was standing out on the curb pointing up at her house. Their other neighbor Randall approached.

"Looks like a few neighbors' lights are out," he said.

Charlotte pressed her palm against her forehead, blowing a sigh of relief. She walked outside and joined them near the curb.

"What's going on?" she asked. "Have we all lost power?"

"That's what it looks like." Linda sighed. "But our houses are the only three on the block that appear to be hit."

"Hmm. That's weird. Has anyone called the electric company yet?"

"My wife just did," Randall said. "Do you have a flashlight? Or candles?"

"I have both. I was so thrown off when the lights went out that I didn't grab either."

Linda handed Charlotte a pink bedazzled flashlight. "Do you want to borrow mine while you go back inside to grab yours?"

"No. I'll be fine. If I can't find the flashlight I keep in the kitchen, I'll just grab one from the trunk of my car."

"Randall!" his wife called out from their front lawn. "I just got a text from the electric company. They're on the way. They should be able to get us back up and running in no time."

"Great. Thanks, hon!"

A cool breeze settled over Charlotte, giving her a sense of calm. "I'm so relieved that this was a mini blackout, and not an attack on me." She paused when her neighbors threw her looks of concern. "I mean, you know, with me being a police sergeant and all, you never know if someone could have something against me, or…"

Linda slowly backed away. "I'm gonna go back home and make sure the kids are okay."

"Yeah, me, too," Randall chimed in. "Hopefully it won't be too much longer before NV Energy gets here."

Charlotte waved sheepishly, embarrassed after realizing that she'd said too much. "Stay safe!" she called out to their backs as they hurried off.

That wasn't much better…

She went inside and closed the door, blinking rapidly as her eyes adjusted to the darkness.

Maybe I should've taken Linda up on that offer to use her flashlight.

The back of her cream leather couch appeared in the distance. Charlotte tiptoed toward it, gliding her hand along the edge on her way to the kitchen.

She stopped at the sound of footsteps stomping across the floor.

What the…

"Miles?" she called out. "Is that you?"

Silence.

That feeling of dread came rushing back. She thought about her gun. It was still in the kitchen.

Dammit!

The footsteps were now clumping through the hallway. Charlotte felt her way toward a corner in the living room and crouched down. Her eyes were fixated on the white walls. A shadowy figure hovered near the living room's entrance. The silhouette's hand slowly rose to his head. He appeared to be holding a gun.

"Chaaarlotte," a shrill voice called out. "Come out, come out wherever you arrreee."

She covered her mouth, stifling a scream. Charlotte wanted to crawl underneath her console table but feared she'd make too much noise. So she sank farther down, praying the blackout would help to hide her.

A stream of light shone into the living room. It bounced from wall to wall like a disco ball, disorienting her as she followed the beam. The clumping soles commenced, moving in closer until the intruder was inside the living room.

Through the darkness, Charlotte could see that he was wearing a ski mask and dark clothing. His feet were covered in black combat boots. A flash of silver in his left hand confirmed that he was, in fact, gripping a gun.

"I found your Glock inside your purse," he whispered, attempting to disguise his voice. "As you very well know, I'm no gunslinger. Shooting victims isn't my modus operandi. But *oh* how satisfying would it be to pop you in the head with your own weapon. I'd hold on to it as a souvenir afterward. And if River Valley PD wanted it returned? They'd have to get it back in blood."

He stopped. Rested against the railing. Then switched off the flashlight. The room went completely dark.

"So, what'll it be, Charlotte? A bullet to the head? Or do you finally wanna find out how I murder my victims? That's what you and your idiotic cohorts have been dying to know, isn't it?"

She dug her fingernails into her calves, racking her brain for a way to escape. If she tried to run for it,

Charlotte knew the man would shoot her right there on the spot.

"Hey!" he yelled. "Are you listening to me?"

She screamed, unable to hold it in any longer.

"Ahh, there she is. I finally got a rise out of the goody-goody, newly minted *Sergeant* Charlotte Bowman. Where's your little bodyguard tonight? Did he get sick of your failure to catch me and back out of the investigation? If he did, who could blame him? River Valley PD is *pathetic*. Especially now that it's being run by the likes of you."

As he rambled on, Charlotte stared up at the silver ballerina statue sitting on the edge of the console table. It appeared blurry through her tears. She considered grabbing it, charging the intruder and ramming it upside his head.

But then she thought otherwise. A bullet would reach her before she reached him.

How in the hell am I going to get out of this?

"Ooh, this is fun!" the man said. "When I cut those power lines, I had *no* idea taunting you would feel this good."

"You're *sick*!" Charlotte uttered. "Why are you doing this?"

The man began pacing the floor. "Why am I doing this? Because I want you to suffer, just like I did!"

He bolted across the room. His knee struck the edge of the coffee table, but he managed to stay on his feet. Charlotte jumped up and tried to run. He dived over the love seat and grabbed the back of her dress, tossing her to the floor. She groaned in pain, rolling over and pulling herself up onto her elbows.

Charlotte could hear the man wheezing as he stomped back and forth.

"See what you made me do? I didn't wanna attack you yet! I'm trying to relish in your fear. I wanna hear it. Smell it. *Taste* it."

She waited for him to turn around and pace toward the window. When his back was to her, she hopped up, grabbed the ballerina statue and struck him across the head.

"Ow!" he hollered, falling onto the couch.

She darted across the room. But he stuck his leg out and tripped her before she could get away. Charlotte grabbed hold of an end table, spun around and kicked him in the groin.

Her foot barely made contact. He grabbed her ankle and twisted it until she fell to her knees.

"This isn't going as planned," he grunted, climbing on top of her. "Now I'm gonna have to kill you!"

Charlotte felt the cold metal tip of the gun graze her left temple. "No, no, no," she muttered, shuddering underneath the weight of his body.

"No, no, no," he mocked, sliding the barrel along her jawline, her neck, then her chest. "How do you want to die, Charlotte? A bullet to the head? To the heart? Or should I just strangle you with my bare hands? I think I'd enjoy that method the most. The feel of your throat constricting in my grasp while your eyes bulge and your body convulses…"

His hand gripped her neck. It was covered in a latex glove.

So no fingerprints. He's going to kill me, and there will be no evidence left behind…

The attacker's jagged fingernails poked through the thin rubber, digging into her flesh. "I wonder how long it'll take you to die once I start squeezing the life out of you. Two minutes? Three minutes? But wait, you're a feisty one, sooo… *Five* minutes?"

Charlotte choked as his grasp tightened. Her eyelids fluttered. Breathing shallowed.

Hold on. Don't give in. Hold on…

She sputtered as a tiny stream of air caught in her throat. Just as she felt herself passing out, a pair of headlights flashed through the window.

Her attacker's grip loosened. After a few moments, the front door opened slightly.

"Thanks, Linda! I'll let Charlotte know that your power is back on and ours should be next."

Miles!

The killer leapt to his feet. Her gun fell from his hand and slid underneath the couch as he ran to the back of the house.

"Miles!" Charlotte attempted to scream. She barely had any voice left.

"Charlotte?" Miles called out.

"Here," she gasped. "Down here!"

He shined his flashlight along the floor, then rushed toward her. "Charlotte! What happened to you?"

She took in a deep breath and exhaled, crying out, "The killer! He was here!"

"He was *here*?" Miles asked, helping her stand. "When?"

"Just now! He ran to the back of the house."

Miles wrapped his arm around her and drew his gun. He handed Charlotte the flashlight, then led her to the kitchen. The back door was wide open. They rushed out onto the deck. The yard was empty. The wooden gate leading to the alleyway swung in the wind.

"He's gone. I let him get away!" Charlotte sobbed, collapsing against Miles.

"This is not your fault. Whichever officer was scheduled to sit out front and keep an eye on things should've been here, watching over the house. Let's go call the station and report this—"

"Wait, Miles. There's something I have to tell you. Officer Haney was scheduled to be here tonight. But… I told him it wasn't necessary."

"Why would you do that?"

Charlotte clutched his arm and led him back inside. "We need to talk. I've got a lot to share with you. And I have a new lead on a suspect."

Chapter Seventeen

Miles handed Charlotte a hot cup of green tea, then took a seat next to her on the couch.

"Thank you," she mumbled.

Charlotte didn't look up from her lap. Miles figured she was too embarrassed to make eye contact after admitting that she'd gone to Hunter's party.

He'd had a strong urge to get back to her after wrapping up his work in Clemmington. So he hopped on the first flight to Nevada without even bothering to unpack or to let her know he was coming. Good thing he followed his gut.

"You know I'm holding back on just how upset I am with you, right?" Miles asked.

"I do. And I appreciate it. Because I don't have it in me to be reprimanded right now—"

"But, Charlotte," he interrupted, "you have got to stop with these rogue solo missions. Seriously."

"I know. And I will."

"Are you sure you don't wanna go to the hospital, just to get checked out and make sure everything's okay?"

"No. I'm fine. I'd rather be out there with the rest of law enforcement, searching for the killer."

"Well, Chief Mitchell wants you to take the night off. Focus on your mental health while they do the heavy lifting."

"I wish I could've gotten a better look at the guy. But he was covered from head to toe and disguising his voice. Plus, it was pitch-black in here. I was completely caught off guard..."

Miles sat back and took a sip of his rum and Coke. "I can't believe the turn this case has taken after that night we were..."

"Together," Charlotte finished after his voice trailed off. "I agree." Her head fell against the back of the couch. "I am juggling so many emotions right now. I'm exhausted yet riled up, discombobulated but laser focused, terrified but feeling fearless. I think I should call Chief Mitchell and tell him that I'm fine. I need to hit the streets and help look for—"

"No, you don't." Miles ran his thumb along the edge of his highball glass, struggling to keep calm despite his anger. "Listen, you've had a long, rough day. It's late, and you're tired. The last thing you should be trying to do is jump into investigation mode after what you went through tonight."

Charlotte sighed, her expression softening. "You know what? You're right."

"I am?" he asked, shocked that she agreed.

"Yes. You usually are."

Her eyes fell to her lap as she fiddled with a cushion zipper. Charlotte wasn't the fidgety type. Something was on her mind.

"What are you not saying to me that you want to say?" Miles asked.

"How is it that you know me so well?"

"I guess I've been around you long enough to sense when something's on your mind. Is it?"

"Yes," Charlotte replied softly. "It is."

"I'm listening."

She sat straight up, running her hands along the sides of her legs. "Full disclosure, when you left for Clemmington, I felt something that I didn't expect to feel."

"Something meaning…"

"Something personal. Emotional. And that got me to thinking about us actually being together."

"Really? I—I'm surprised to hear that. Especially after the conversation we had outside of the medical examiner's office. What brought this on?"

"Having you here in River Valley has enabled me to see you in a different light. The way you go to such great lengths to protect me and make sure I'm okay. That is one of the most attractive traits a man could have."

"It comes naturally. Because I really care about you."

"And I really care about you, too, Miles. But I've found myself fighting my feelings. Because this time around, it's not a divorce that's standing in my way. It's this investigation. I'm so focused on capturing this killer that I can't see beyond it. Plus, what if we got involved and people in the department found out? Chief Mitchell already thinks my head isn't in the game. A relationship between us would only add to that theory. And even if we start something up and try to keep it a secret, that would be too much pressure. Can you understand what I'm saying?"

"I can. My heart says otherwise, but I get it. I came here to help you solve this case. That hasn't changed.

Now, do I wish something more could happen between us? Of course. Because my feelings for you aren't going away. But at the same time, I do realize our focus needs to remain on the investigation."

She leaned in and kissed him tenderly on the cheek. "Thank you for that. And who knows what may happen once the killer is behind bars."

"Don't make any promises you can't keep."

Charlotte pinched his nose. "That wasn't a promise. It was simply a statement."

He reached over and ran his fingertips along her throat. "How does your neck feel? Still sore?"

"A little. But the pain is easing up."

"Good." Miles drained his glass, then stood. "I think I need a refill. Can I get you another cup of tea?"

"No, thanks. But you can pour me a rum and Coke, too. I think it's time for something a little stronger."

"You got it."

Charlotte's cell phone buzzed.

"Can you get that?" she asked him. "I'm too tired to get up."

"Sure. We should probably check in with Chief Mitchell. See if any officers were able to find Hunter, or spot someone who may be linked to your attack."

"Good idea."

Miles grabbed her phone off the mantel and tapped the text notification. A message from an anonymous number popped up on the screen, bolded and in all caps.

TRUST THAT I'M COMING BACK FOR YOU, SERGEANT CHARLOTTE BOWMAN! NEXT TIME, THERE WILL BE NO INTERRUPTIONS. I'LL BE COMING IN HOT. GUNS BLAZING!

His mouth went dry as he reread the message.

"Oh, no," Charlotte groaned. "You look like you're about to be sick. What is it?"

Miles handed her the phone. "Another threat."

She read the text, then sprang to her feet. "*I'm coming in hot, I'm coming in hot...* Where have I heard that? Hold on!" Charlotte pulled up the video she'd filmed at Hunter's party.

"What is this?" Miles asked.

"Just watch."

He looked on as an image of Hunter climbing onto a balcony appeared.

"I'm coming in hot!" Hunter yelled before diving into the pool.

Charlotte stood frigidly, visibly shaking. She stopped the video and dialed Chief Mitchell's number. "We need to bring Hunter in for questioning. *Immediately.*"

Chapter Eighteen

Officer Haney escorted Hunter inside the interrogation room.

"I found him passed out on his front lawn," the policeman said. "Brought him straight here."

Charlotte rolled her eyes at the sight of Hunter, dressed in nothing but yellow swim trunks and flip-flops. His bare, muscular chest was completely sunburned, as were his peeling cheeks. One of his puffy eyes had been blackened, and his lower lip was split open.

Hunter winced as he walked toward the chair across from her and Miles. Charlotte peeked down at his inner thighs. Just as she'd suspected, they were covered in bright red scrapes, along with his stomach and arms.

Shouldn't have been climbing up that palm tree, idiot...

"Have a seat, Mr. Stout," Miles said.

He slammed down into the chair. "Ooh," he moaned, pressing his hands against his legs.

"Long night, huh?" Charlotte asked, surprised that his attorney wasn't there with him.

"Yeah. A long night that never ended." Hunter

squinted, covering his eyes while staring up at the ceiling. "Is there any way you could turn down those fluorescent lights?"

"This is a police station," Miles said. "Not a spa. The lights aren't on dimmers."

"What the hell am I doing here, anyway? Is this about Stephen's murder? I already told Chief Mitchell everything I could remember about the night he went missing—"

"This isn't about Stephen's murder," Charlotte interrupted. "At least not yet." She slid a photo of Nalah across the table. "Do you recognize this woman?"

The black plastic chair that Hunter was sitting on wobbled back and forth as he scooted closer. "Um, she looks a little familiar. But I don't know. I have a lot of parties at my house. She may have stopped through one or two of them."

Charlotte studied his broad shoulders and tone of voice, wondering if he was the man who'd attacked her last night.

"What about now?" she continued, slamming a photo of Hunter at Nalah's crime scene down in front of him. "Do you remember seeing her at Angler Canyon Reservoir the day she turned up dead?"

His mouth fell open. A shallow gasp was all he could muster.

"What were you doing out there?" Miles asked.

Hunter rubbed his hands together, then ran them up and down his scruffy beard. "I, um… Wait. It's starting to come back to me now…"

"*What's* starting to come back to you?"

"How I know her."

Several moments of silence passed.

"Are you planning to share that information with us sometime today?" Charlotte asked.

Hunter slid down in his chair and crossed his arms over his chest. "Yeah. She was dating one of my boys."

Charlotte glanced over at Miles, wondering if Hunter was referring to Josh or Rob. "Which one of your boys?"

Another long pause.

"Answer the questions, Hunter," Miles insisted.

"T-Tom," he muttered underneath his breath.

"Who?"

"Tom," he repeated a little louder.

"As in Tommy?"

He shrugged. "Yeah. I guess."

"So you're friends with Tommy," Charlotte said, nudging Miles. "Funny, Tommy never mentioned that to us."

"It is, isn't it? And the perfect opportunity would've been that day we all saw Hunter at the Razzle Dazzle."

"You saw me at the strip club?"

Charlotte held up her hand. "We're not here to answer your questions. Now, where were you last night?"

Hunter sat straight up and looked her in the eyes. "I was at my parents' vacation house. Throwing a party. And you know what's funny? I saw an uninvited guest there who looked just like you."

"Oh, did you? Hmm. That's interesting. You must have me mistaken for someone else. But you know what's even funnier than what you *think* you saw? The fact that I was attacked last night by a man who looked just like you!" Charlotte retorted, knowing she was exaggerating but wanting to see his reaction.

"You were *what*?" Hunter yelled, leaping to his feet.

"Hey, sit down!" Miles commanded. "Before I have Officer Haney come back in here and place you under arrest."

"For what?"

"Disorderly conduct, for starters. Now, do we need to have you restrained?"

"No," Hunter mumbled, slinking back down into his chair. "Look," he said to Charlotte, "I didn't attack you. I was at the house all night, up until that stupid ass policeman picked me up and brought me here."

"Can you prove to us that you didn't leave?" Charlotte asked.

"Yes. I have hundreds of eyewitnesses who can vouch for me."

"What about the security cameras? And your neighbors' cameras? Will the footage tell us a different story?"

Hunter didn't respond. Miles held his hand to his ear and leaned into the table. "I'm sorry, Mr. Stout. I don't think I heard you. What was that you said?"

He pushed forward in his chair, balancing himself on its two front legs. "I didn't say anything…"

"And why is that?"

"Because you all are trying to pin something on me that I didn't do! And I *may* have left the house for a few minutes or whatever. But the reason why isn't any of your business."

"The hell it isn't," Charlotte shot back. "The reason why you left could have you serving a twenty-year sentence for attempted murder."

"Or multiple life sentences if you had anything to

do with all the other murders that've recently taken place," Miles added.

"Wait a minute!" Hunter roared. "Are you actually accusing me of being a damn *serial* killer?"

Charlotte pulled her cell phone out of her navy blazer pocket and opened the video of Hunter jumping into the pool. "Is this you?"

"See!" he exclaimed, bouncing up and down in his seat. "I knew that was you at my party!"

"Answer the question! Is this you?"

Hunter flopped back so hard that his chair almost toppled over. "Yes! It's me. And you already know that. So why are you asking?"

"This phrase that you used before jumping into the pool, *I'm coming in hot.* Is that something you say on a regular basis?"

"I don't know. I guess. Why?"

Charlotte pulled up the text sent to her by the killer. "Did you send this to me?"

Hunter's eyes darted across the screen, his lips moving as he read the message. "No. I didn't. *I'm coming in hot* is a popular hip hop phrase. People use it all the time. And I hate to break it to you, but I'm not the nut-job killer you're looking for. Sorry you two can't seem to get the job done and catch him, but you're coming after the wrong guy."

"But you admit that there was a time during the party when you went missing," Charlotte reiterated. "Where did you go?"

"To buy drugs, okay? Are you happy now? And don't even bother trying to find out who my dealer is, because I'll never tell."

"Would you be willing to let us take a look at your cell phone?" Miles asked.

"Yeah. I would. Because my biggest secret is out of the bag now. I do drugs. Can you arrest me for that?"

"Do you have any on you?"

"Nope."

"Then let's just focus on you handing over that phone. We've got bigger things to deal with right now."

Hunter snatched the cell out of his pocket and slid it across the table. "Open the camera roll at your own risk. There may be a sex tape or two in there."

"Believe me," Charlotte mumbled as she scrolled through his text messages, "we are not interested in seeing that."

Nothing in his phone appeared suspicious. Just messages to and from family and friends. Charlotte stood and handed him the cell.

"Hunter, please excuse us. We'll be right back." She gestured for Miles to follow her out. As soon as the door closed behind them, Charlotte breathed a sigh of frustration.

"I don't think it's him," she said.

"Are you sure?"

"Not a hundred percent. But my gut is telling me that it isn't."

"I don't think we should let up on him just yet."

Charlotte threw her arms out at her sides. "Well, we can't hold him. We don't have anything on him."

"True. Let's shift our focus, then. Follow up with Tommy and see if he'll admit to selling drugs to Hunter."

"That, plus we need to follow up on that Ring camera footage he never turned over."

Miles nodded, brushing a stray curl behind Charlotte's ear. "How are you feeling? You doing okay?"

"I am. I'm feeling pretty strong."

"Glad to hear it. Should we go back in and tell Hunter he's free to go?"

"Yes, we should." She hesitated. "Miles, I know you've heard this from me before, but I have to say it again. Thank you for being here. I could not have gotten through any of this without you. Actually, I wouldn't even be here right now if it weren't for you."

"Once again, you do not have to keep thanking me. There is nowhere else I'd rather be. And you're welcome."

When Officer Haney walked by, Miles signaled him over. Charlotte instructed the policeman to swab Hunter's cheek for DNA, then take him home.

On the way out, Hunter approached her and Miles.

"You all need to talk to Tommy. He's the one who had me out at that crime scene. Before you two even got there."

"How do you know that?" Charlotte asked.

"Because I saw you running up the canyon, past the caution tape, while I was out in the crowd. How did Tommy know that Nalah had been killed, *and* where to find her body, so early in the game?"

Charlotte stood silently for several moments, then instructed Officer Haney to take him away.

"What's our next move?" Miles asked, following her down the hallway.

"It's time to pay Tommy a visit."

"I agree. If he doesn't have that security camera footage, we should arrest him right there on the spot. We've got enough probable cause, especially considering he was the last person seen with Nalah the night she went missing."

"And I won't even bother asking a judge for a warrant. We'll just take him right into custody."

Chapter Nineteen

Miles made a left turn onto Buckhorn Lane and tapped the brake. He jerked the steering wheel, barely missing a huge ball of tumbleweed rolling across the road.

"This literally looks like a scene straight out of an old Western," Charlotte muttered.

After leaving the police station, she and Miles drove to Tommy's house. He wasn't there, so they tried Candy's apartment. Neither of them were there. They figured the pair must be at the Razzle Dazzle and headed straight to the club.

Miles pulled into the parking lot. It was packed, as usual. There appeared to be some sort of commotion near the entrance. He stopped the car and saw Tommy shove the old rocker who manned the door against a wooden railing. Candy attempted to squeeze her skinny body in between them. Tommy pushed her away, knocking her to the ground.

"Hey!" Charlotte yelled, bolting from the car and running toward them. "What is going on out here?"

"Buster is tryna charge me thirty dollars to get inside the club!" Tommy yelled before pushing him again.

"I already told you," Buster heaved, his gravelly

voice barely audible, "no more freebies! Your tab is already over a thousand dollars!"

"Man, go to hell—"

Before Tommy could finish, Buster grabbed him by his wifebeater's straps and slammed him against the splintered front door.

"That's enough!" Miles said, pulling the men apart.

Just as Buster bent down and dusted off his jeans, Tommy lunged at him. His fist almost clipped Buster's jaw, but the old rocker ducked right before it connected. The miss caused Tommy to lose his footing. He stumbled across the cedar decking board and hit the floor. On the way down, a small plastic bag fell from his pocket.

"Ohh," Charlotte breathed as Miles restrained him. She grabbed the bag and studied the powdery white substance inside. "What do we have here, Tommy?"

He rolled over onto his side and clutched his rib cage.

"Tommy," Charlotte repeated. "What is this?"

"Baking soda," he moaned.

She handed the bag to Miles. "How much are you willing to bet that Tommy is Hunter's drug dealer?"

"Not a dime. Because I don't like to lose, and that would be like handing over free money."

Candy bent down and cradled Tommy's head in her hands. "You okay, baby?"

"No. I think I'm dying!"

Buster stepped over his body and threw open the door. "I'm going back inside to call the police."

"Sir," Miles said, "we are the police."

"Good! Then arrest this asswipe for attempted murder!"

"I don't think we can go that far," Charlotte said. "But he will be coming with us. Get up, Tommy. Let's go."

"*Let's go.* Go where?"

"Down to the police station."

He rolled over onto his other side and cried out, "I think I need an ambulance. Take me to the hospital!"

Miles grabbed him by the arm and pulled him to his feet.

"Careful!" Tommy shouted. "My arm feels like it's broken. And most of my ribs, too. *Owww.*"

"Candy!" Buster yelled. "You'd better get your butt back in here before you lose your job. The DJ is calling you to the stage!"

She grabbed Tommy's face and showered it with kisses. "I gotta go, baby. Are you coming back when you're done with the cops?"

"Wait," Tommy whined. "You're not coming with me to the station?"

"I can't, babe. My big performance with Nikki Nonstop is tonight. Plus a few of my regulars are here, and I owe them—"

"I don't give a damn who's here! I need you!"

"All right," Miles said. "That's enough. Let's go."

"Bye, cuddles!" Candy called out, blowing kisses in the air. "I love you!"

"No, you don't!" Tommy cried. "If you did, you wouldn't be abandoning me right now. It's so obvious that love don't live here anymore."

Charlotte stopped Buster before he went back inside. "Are you okay, sir?"

"Yeah. I'm good. But I'll be even better once that

punk pays the club what he owes us. Yo!" he shouted in Tommy's direction. "Just in case you hadn't guessed it, you're officially banned from the Razzle Dazzle until you pay up!"

Charlotte caught up with Miles as he placed Tommy in the back of the car.

"So," Miles said to him, "whatever happened to that Ring camera footage you were supposed to turn over to us?"

Tommy didn't respond.

"Trust me," the detective continued, "now is not the time to go silent. You've got a lot of explaining to do. And you'll have plenty of time to do it once we get inside that interrogation room."

"PLEASE, DETECTIVE LOVELACE," Tommy begged. *"Please!"*

Miles glared in the rearview mirror. "It's Detective Love. And we do not have time to stop by your house. We've already shown you more than enough grace. The niceties stop here."

Charlotte turned in her seat, watching as Tommy broke down in tears. "How much time did we give you to turn over that footage?"

He rolled his neck, staring out the window rather than responding.

"*A lot.* My guess is that you don't have it. Because if you did, you would have handed it over by now. Apparently, it's more important for you to start fights at a strip club with drugs in your pocket than to prove your innocence in a murder investigation."

"Exactly," Miles agreed. "Therefore, to the police station we go."

A loud bang echoed through the car. Charlotte spun back around. Tommy was slamming his head against the window, cursing under his breath.

"Do you want me to have you committed under an involuntary seventy-two-hour hold?" Miles threatened.

"No! I'm just... I'm *frustrated*. Because I dropped the ball and didn't send you that damn footage. But I'm in love, dude! Can't you understand that?"

"Please!" Charlotte shouted. "For the last time, it's Detective Love. Not *dude*. Show some respect."

"Sorry, *Detective Love*. Anyway, like I was saying, I'm in love. Candy's got me outta my head. Like, in a chokehold or something."

"Candy?" Miles asked. "Or cocaine?"

"Du—I mean Detective, I am not on coke. Come on. Just give me a chance to prove what I'm saying is true. Take me to my house and let me pull up the footage. I promise that'll show you I wasn't involved in Nalah's murder."

"You know," Charlotte cut in, "you keep proclaiming your innocence. If you really are, then how did you know Nalah was dead so early on in the investigation and where her body could be found?"

"What are you talking about?" Tommy asked.

"Hunter told us that you were the one who informed him of Nalah's murder and sent him to the crime scene."

"That snitch," he muttered under his breath. "Look, here's the deal. There's an underground group of guys who listen to River Valley's police scanner faithfully. Hunter and I are both in it. Whenever a call comes in to 9-1-1 reporting a crime, at least one of us rushes to the scene to film it for our YouTube channel."

"Your *YouTube* channel?" Miles repeated. "Ugh, that is ridiculous. Sounds to me like you all have way too much time on your hands."

"Don't knock it. We've got over a hundred thousand subscribers, and we're making a whole lotta money off all our sponsors and ads. But anyway, the day that Nalah's body was found, I couldn't make it to the scene because I was, uh…*preoccupied* with Candy. So Hunter went instead. At the time, I didn't even realize that it was Nalah out there. We just knew a body had been found. And obviously we heard the location being transmitted over the scanner."

"This case is getting stranger and stranger by the day," Charlotte said. "So, this YouTube channel. What's the name of it?"

"The Hunter and the Hunted. Get it? It's like, we're on the hunt for crime scenes, and the victims have been hunted down by some perp. The name is a play on words, too, since Hunter is a founding member of the group. See what we did there?"

Miles snapped his fingers. "Yeah, back to Hunter. Why didn't you tell us that you know him so well the day he showed up at the Razzle Dazzle?"

"Because, you know my motto. Snitches get stitches. So what's up? Don't you wanna free me so you can go after the real killer? All you gotta do is turn the car around, slide through my crib and let me show you that video footage!"

Miles tapped his fist against the steering wheel. Tension crept up his neck as his temples ached with frustration. "What do you think?" he asked Charlotte. "Should we take a quick detour and stop by his house?"

"Yes!" Tommy hollered. "Let's do it!"

Charlotte ignored him. "It wouldn't hurt. For once, Tommy actually has a point. If he can prove that he returned home that night—"

"Which I did," he interrupted.

"—and stayed there until the next day," she continued, "then we can check him off our list of suspects."

"Might as well. At this point, what do we have to lose?" Miles glanced in the rearview mirror. "Tommy, you'd better not be wasting our time."

The detective made a U-turn and sped down Beaumont Street.

"If he is guilty," Charlotte whispered, "he's doing a great job of hiding it. Because if nothing else, the man is confident."

"Yeah, let's see how confident he is once he gets behind the computer and has to pull up that footage."

When they arrived at the house, Tommy skipped up the walkway as if he didn't have a care in the world. The second he opened the door, Charlotte and Miles were hit with the stench of musty clothes mixed with stale marijuana smoke.

Black curtains were drawn, making it almost impossible to see through the living room. But the clutter was apparent. Take-out containers, cardboard boxes and dirty dishes were strewn everywhere. A futon, folding chair and set of crates acting as a coffee table were the only pieces of furniture in the room.

"Are you in the process of moving out?" Miles asked.

"Nah. Candy hates the place, so I boxed up a bunch of my stuff so we could do some decorating." Tommy pointed at the futon. "Have a seat. I'll go grab my laptop. Can I get you all something to drink? Alls I've got is beer, Red Bull and hard seltzer. And tap water."

"No, thank you," Charlotte replied, holding her finger to her nose. "Just go get your computer so we can grab the footage and get out of here."

A peeling plaid blanket covered the futon. Miles and Charlotte threw one another looks of disgust before sitting as close to the edge as possible.

"This little pit stop had better be worth it," he warned.

"Agreed. I'm beginning to feel nauseous."

Tommy shuffled back into the room with his computer. He plopped down in between Miles and Charlotte and logged into his Ring account.

"All righty," he said, rubbing his hands together. "Here we go."

Tommy clicked on the History tab. Nothing appeared on the screen. "Wait," he mumbled, hitting the enter button on the keyboard. Still nothing. "What the hell is happening right now?" He pounded the touchpad, then the enter key, then the touchpad again.

"Where are your recorded videos?" Miles asked.

"I don't know. I must be doing something wrong here. I've never tried to go back and review old footage. I usually only watch the live views."

"Hold on," Charlotte said. "Tommy, do you have a Ring protection plan?"

"No. It costs extra. Why?"

"Because that's what you need in order to record surveillance footage! If you don't have a protection plan, then your camera won't tape anything. It only streams live videos." She headed for the door. "Miles, cuff him so we can get down to the station and move forward with the interrogation. I also wanna run the drugs he had on him through a chemical test kit so we'll know whether it's cocaine, or heroin, or—"

"Hold on," Tommy said. "It's none of those things! And I can prove it!"

Miles waved him off. "Here we go with the false promises again. Just like you were gonna prove via surveillance footage that you were here with Candy all night when Nalah went missing, right?"

"Wrong."

Tommy scrambled to his feet and ran to the back of the house. Charlotte and Miles chased after him.

"Where are you going?" she yelled.

"To the bathroom! The proof is in my medicine cabinet!"

The pair stood outside of the cramped powder room, watching as Tommy knocked every bottle inside the cabinet into the sink. "It's here," he panted. "Somewhere…"

"What's here?" Miles asked.

"The meds that are in that baggie you all confiscated!"

The detective stepped over the threshold, struggling to avoid brushing up against the filthy pedestal sink. "You know what? That's enough. Your time is up. Let's go." He pulled a pair of handcuffs from his back pocket.

"Wait!" Tommy said, shoving a bottle in Miles's face. "See? Here it is. Those are not illegal drugs in that bag. It's crushed up OxyContin. I've got a prescription. My name is on it and everything."

Miles grabbed the bottle and handed it to Charlotte, then handcuffed him.

"Come on, man!" he cried.

"Detective Love," Miles reiterated, pushing him out of the bathroom.

"Come on, Detective Love! And Captain Berkin!"

They ignored him, hauling Tommy out to the car.

"I'm gonna prove you both wrong," he grumbled. "Watch me."

"Yeah, well, until then," Charlotte said, "you'll be in police custody."

An elderly woman stood on the curb across the street, checking her mailbox. "Hello, Tommy," she called out. "Thank you so much for mowing my lawn this morning."

"You're welcome," Tommy responded, barely looking up at her. Right before he climbed inside the car, he popped back up.

"What are you doing?" Miles asked.

"Just gimme a second. Hey! Mrs. Milton?"

"Yes?"

"Don't you have a Ring surveillance system?"

"A what?"

"A Ring camera security system!"

"I do. Why?"

"Does your camera record video footage?"

"I think so."

"Where are you going with this?" Charlotte asked him.

"Mrs. Milton lives directly across the street from my house. Her camera may have recorded me the night Nalah went missing."

Miles grabbed the top of Tommy's head and nudged him toward the back seat. "That's quite a long shot. Too bad you weren't that interested in retrieving the footage when we initially requested it."

Tommy pushed back, resisting Miles's effort to get him inside the car. "Mrs. Milton! If you can pull up footage of me from two weeks ago, call and let me know!"

The woman stepped into the street. "From two weeks ago? I'll see what I can do, hon. Is everything all right?"

"Everything is fine, ma'am," Charlotte said. "Thank you." She nodded in Miles's direction. "Come on. Let's hurry up and get him to the station."

Chapter Twenty

Miles clutched the steering wheel as he drove toward Charlotte's house. After another long, exhausting day at the station, the pair were finally heading home.

It'd been nearly three weeks since Nalah's murder, and the investigation had been inundated with false leads. Intense pressure was closing in on the entire force. But no one felt it more deeply than Charlotte, which caused tensions to build between her and Miles.

"Once again," she began, her tone trembling with frustration, "we need to meet with Chief Mitchell and share our suspicions about Walter."

Choose your words wisely, Miles told himself.

"Charlotte, I know you're anxious to tell the chief what you think you know about Walter's involvement in—"

"What I *think* I know? Come on, Miles. The writing's on the wall. This investigation has hit one dead end after another. Every other suspect on our list has checked out. All roads lead back to Walter. *Now's* the time for us to put together a formal report and present it to Chief Mitchell first thing in the morning."

Miles let up on the accelerator as he turned down

Charlotte's block. "I still think you're jumping the gun. We'll only get one shot to explain why we think the corporal of River Valley PD is a serial killer. When we do, our presentation has got to be well-thought-out and chock-full of facts."

"And it will be. Now let's go inside and get to work!"

"No," Miles argued, "it won't be. We still don't have enough evidence to prove Walter's guilt."

Charlotte reached for her door handle as he pulled in front of the house. Before he could bring the car to a complete stop, she jumped out.

"Really?" Miles asked. "So you're just gonna storm off rather than talk things out?"

"Yes! Because this conversation is over," Charlotte shot back before rushing up the walkway.

Miles sat there, his head falling against the back of the seat.

"I can't do this," he muttered before driving off.

THIRTY MINUTES LATER, the detective found himself turning into Angler Canyon Reservoir's parking lot. Miles took his time before climbing out of the car. His calf muscles stiffened as he stood—the result of spending way more time behind a desk than in the gym.

The setting sun cooled the air blowing through the canyon. He rolled up the sleeves on his pale blue shirt and inhaled, almost tasting the fragrant white flowers blooming from lush ash trees. Miles was grateful for the much-needed time alone, even if it was being spent at a crime scene.

Despite Charlotte's angry delivery, she'd been right about one thing—their investigation had certainly been hit with one dead end after another. All of the victims' autopsy and toxicology reports came back negative for foreign substances. Neither Tommy's nor Hunter's DNA matched evidence at the crime scenes, and their You-Tube channel checked out. Results from the forensic sweep performed on Charlotte's house the night she was attacked came back inconclusive.

Law enforcement was able to retrieve surveillance footage from the night of Hunter's party that showed him leaving and returning to the property. But he hadn't been gone long enough to have assaulted Charlotte. Ironically, his drug dealer alibied him, admitting that he'd sold marijuana to Hunter at the reported time.

The powdery white substance they'd confiscated from Tommy turned out to be oxycodone, just as he'd claimed. His neighbor Mrs. Milton handed over the Ring camera footage from the night Nalah went missing. Just as he'd claimed, it showed Tommy and Candy entering his home that evening and reemerging the following day.

Once Hunter and Tommy were cleared, Charlotte and Miles had grilled Walter on whether he'd told Josh that Stephen's cell phone was in police custody. Walter denied it, and Chief Mitchell believed him. When Charlotte asked Walter what happened to the inside information he'd sworn he could pull from Stephen's friends, she discovered they'd cut him off after rumors swirled he was trying to frame them. Nevertheless, the chief refused to question Walter's integrity.

Maybe all that is what brought me out here, Miles thought. Because at this point, he was willing to do whatever it took to solve the case so he could return to

Clemmington. Even if it meant scouring crime scenes alone. Because being in such close quarters with the woman he cared about yet continually clashed with was becoming too much to bear.

The detective trekked down the rocky terrain toward a cluster of sagebrush shrubs nestled in the hillside. It was the exact spot where Nalah's body had been found. Wind whipped across the canyon, breezing through tree leaves as sunlight slipped behind the mountains. Chirping songbirds and gurgling waves made for serene surroundings. Most fishermen, boaters and sunbathers had already vacated the site. A calm filled the air, contrasting with the violence of the heinous crime that had taken place there weeks ago.

Walter's initial report indicated that just like the other victims, there was no trauma to Nalah's body. But her lavender tank dress had been pulled up around her shoulders, while the rest of the bodies remained fully clothed. She'd been found completely nude from the neck down. According to the medical examiner, she hadn't been sexually assaulted. Charlotte believed the killer left her in that position to taunt the River Valley PD. Miles feared that if they didn't capture him soon, his attacks would come faster and become more brutal.

Kicking a cluster of rocks aside, Miles pulled out his cell and snapped several photos of the shrubs. Just as he zoomed in, it vibrated. The buzz startled him, sending the phone tumbling into a tangle of gray branches.

"Ugh," Miles huffed, scraping his hand as he reached into the jagged twigs and retrieved it.

Charlotte's name flashed across the screen. "Hey,

what's up?" he asked, not bothering to disguise the irritation in his voice.

"Hel-help me..."

Miles shot straight up. "Charlotte? What's wrong?"

She gasped into the phone. And then silence.

"Charlotte!" he yelled, charging back toward the
parking lot. "Are you okay? What's going on?"

"Heee..."

The phone went dead.

Miles jumped inside the car and sped off toward
her house.

WHY DIDN'T YOU *call 9-1-1?*

It was too late now. Miles burst through Charlotte's
front door, rushing from room to room in search of her.

"Charlotte! Where are you?"

Silence.

"Charlotte!"

The stench of burning meat drifted through the house.
Miles ran to the kitchen. It was filled with smoke, but
Charlotte wasn't there. The patio door was open. He ran
outside.

Haze smoldered across the deck. Three feet of fire
burned from the grill. Miles stumbled down the stairs,
choking as fumes filled his lungs.

"Charlotte!"

His eyes stung as he struggled to see. Grabbing a
bag of sand from underneath the deck, he dumped it
onto the grill and put out the fire. Through the billowing smoke, he caught a glimpse of Charlotte.

She was sprawled on the ground with her arms out

at her sides and eyes closed. He rushed over and fell to his knees.

"Char, wake up," he pleaded, pulling her onto his lap. "Come on, wake up!"

She didn't budge. A heightened sense of panic stifled his breathing. He checked her pulse. It was weak.

At least she's alive...

"Who did this to you?" Miles lamented, wrapping her in his arms and rushing her to the hospital.

Chapter Twenty-One

"So, you weren't attacked?" Miles asked Charlotte.

She shook her head, pulling at the cannula tube tangled in the IV line. "No. Or... I don't think so."

He reached across the hospital bed and clutched her hand. "You don't remember what happened? Or how you ended up fainting?"

"Not really. I just know I wanted to surprise you with a special dinner since things have been so strained between us lately. I remember firing up the grill, throwing on the steaks, and then *boom*. I hit the ground, called you, and now I'm here at the hospital."

"Well, first off, thank you for the dinner gesture. I really appreciate you doing that. But I'm so confused. Did someone come in and hit you over the head, and now you can't remember? Or did you get overheated from all the smoke?"

"I just— I don't know." Charlotte pressed her palm against her pounding forehead. "I do feel a migraine coming on, though. And my stomach is killing me."

"It could be that the stress of this case is catching up to you. We'll see what the doctor says once your lab results come back."

The anguish in Miles's unsteady tone was apparent. Charlotte stared into his bloodshot eyes. He looked as though he hadn't slept in days.

"I'm sorry," she whispered.

"For what?"

"For the way I've been treating you. This case has got me bugging out. I know I haven't been the nicest person to deal with. So for that, I apologize."

The hurt that had been riding Miles's shoulders lifted a bit. "Thank you for saying that. And I get it. You're anxious to catch this killer before he commits another murder. You've been attacked. And threatened. Our leads are going cold before they even catch any real steam. It's enough to break anybody's spirit and alter their behavior."

"You're always so diplomatic. And you know all the right things to say." She tightened her hold on his hand. "I'm glad you understand."

The moment was interrupted when Charlotte's cell phone buzzed.

"Can you see who that is?" she asked. "I'm being held captive by all these lines."

"Charlotte, why don't you rest instead of worrying about who's contacting you? You're under enough stress. I don't want you to—"

"Miles," she interrupted. "I don't want a repeat of what happened the last time I ignored my phone. Now please, can you just see who it is?"

A low grunt preceded him grabbing the phone off the wooden nightstand. "It's a text from Chief Mitchell."

"See, there may be something important going on."

She took the phone and scanned the message. "Oh, wow…"

"What did he say?"

"The chief just got a call from the forensics lab. The results came back on that syringe Walter collected from Nalah's crime scene."

"And?"

"There were traces of heroin inside of it. The finger-prints were run through CODIS and matched up with a man named Otis Fielding."

"Does that name ring a bell?" Miles asked.

"It does. Otis is a well-known drug addict here in River Valley who's got a lengthy criminal history. His rap sheet is filled with petty crimes, though. Nothing serious."

"Up until now, possibly. What's the next move? Is he being brought in for questioning?"

"No. Because Otis is in jail right now for attempted armed robbery. He's been locked up for almost three months. There's no way he could have killed Nalah. Angler Canyon is a popular hangout spot for drug addicts. We try and keep the area clean, but they know how to hide within the terrain."

"So in other words, you don't think the syringe is connected to Nalah's murder."

"No. I don't."

Miles nudged her arm. "Why do I get the feeling you're a little pleased with this news?"

"Stop that." She snickered, swatting his hand away. "I just want this case to be solved, even if it is at the hands of Walter. But it won't be."

"I know. Because you're convinced that he's the killer."

"Exactly."

The doctor entered the room. "How are you feeling, Ms. Bowman?"

"A little better, I guess. My head and stomach are still bothering me, but I'm not feeling quite as woozy as I did when I first came in. Maybe I just needed to sit still and get some fluids in my system."

"Could be…" The doctor, who appeared to be in his late sixties, scratched his balding head while shuffling over to the monitor. "Your blood pressure has gone back up since you first arrived, which is a good sign."

"That's a great sign," Miles said. "And by the looks of that big grin on your face, Doc, I'm guessing Charlotte's lab results came back okay?"

"Oh, yes. Ms. Bowman's lab results look good. Really good."

"So what do you think is wrong with me?" she asked. "Why did I fall out like that?"

The doctor held her file to his chest and rocked back on his heels. "The reason you fainted was due to a drop in your blood pressure, which was caused by a hormonal release. When that happens, the blood vessels in the body relax, preventing the proper amount of blood from reaching your brain."

"Okay," Charlotte said slowly. "What does all that mean, then? Am I going into early menopause?"

"Quite the opposite, Ms. Bowman. You're pregnant."

She emitted a cackle so shrill that it rattled her pounding head. "I'm sorry. I thought you said I was pregnant. So, perimenopause, huh? You think that's what's happening here?"

"No, not perimenopause. You are *pregnant*."

The room faded to black. Charlotte's brain buzzed with disbelief. She turned to Miles, blinking rapidly until he came into view. His eyes were bulging out of his head. And his bright smile was filled with joy.

Miles's fingers intertwined with hers. Charlotte's remained limp, unable to grasp his hand or the pregnancy news.

"How far along is she?" he asked.

"Not far, but the gynecologist will talk to her about that," Charlotte thought she'd heard through the white noise ringing in her ears.

Miles moved from the chair to the bed. The corners of his eyes were damp with tears. Every tooth inside his mouth was on full display as he wrapped his arm around her.

"This is…this is unreal!" he exclaimed.

'Yeah," she squeaked. "It sure is."

The doctor patted Charlotte's shoulder. "Congratulations, you two. I'll leave you alone for a bit so you can digest the news. In the meantime, if you need anything, just buzz the nurse and she'll be right in."

"Will do," Miles said. "Thank you, Doctor."

The moment the door closed behind him, Charlotte burst into tears. Miles was holding her so tightly that he didn't seem to notice.

"Please," she gasped. "I can't breathe!"

"Oh! Sorry."

Charlotte grabbed a tissue and cup of ice water, avoiding his gaze. He slowly pulled away.

"You're not happy about the news, are you?" Miles asked.

"I just… I'm *shocked*. This is the last thing I expected. A baby? I'm not prepared to have a baby. I just got promoted to sergeant. I'm in the middle of the biggest investigation of my career. You and I aren't married. We're not even dating—"

"Charlotte," Miles interrupted. "Listen to me. This is a surprise for us both. And I understand how you feel. A baby doesn't fit into your plan. But you know what? I see this as a blessing. A light to brighten all the darkness surrounding us. We're going to bring new life into the world. I hope this doesn't sound selfish, but I've always wanted to be a father. And I can't think of anyone I'd rather share that honor with than you."

Tears trickled down Charlotte's cheeks. Her body grew numb with fear. And doubt. She flung the stiff white blanket off to the side as her entire body began to sweat.

"I hear you, Miles. But you're gonna have to give me some time to process all of this. It's a lot…"

"I know it is. And I will. It goes without saying that I will be here with you every step of the way."

She nodded, unable to respond. He leaned in and kissed her forehead. Overcome by a bout of vulnerability, she rested her head on his chest.

"I've got you," he whispered, stroking her hair. "I've got *us*."

Charlotte thought of Chief Mitchell. If he found out about the pregnancy, he would want to take her off the case.

"I don't want anyone in the department to know about this," she told Miles.

"Not even the chief?"

"*Especially* not the chief. At least not right now. I'll tell him eventually."

"You should. Sooner rather than later. Because obviously this pregnancy is going to affect your involvement in the investigation."

She sat straight up, pulling away from his embrace. "How so?"

"What do you mean, *how so*? The long hours you've been working, the grueling crime scene examinations, visits to the morgue, suspect interrogations—all of those things take a toll on your mental and physical well-being. Not to mention your stress level. Keep in mind what happened to you today. I know you don't wanna hear this, but you're going to have to pull back on this case, Charlotte."

She fell back onto a pillow, pressing her fingertips against her throbbing temples. "Here we go. See, this is what I mean. I'm not ready to stop. Now is not the time to let up on this case, Miles. Pregnant or not, we need to go harder."

"Well, sorry to break it to you, but you can't. I won't let you risk your life or the life of our child for this. There are plenty of capable law enforcement officers in the department who can step up and assist in the investigation."

Charlotte closed her eyes, counting to ten while taking deep breaths. The pain in her stomach began to subside. She placed her hand over her belly as Miles's words replayed in her head.

He was right. This was a blessing. But what should've been the best moment in her life couldn't have come at a worse time.

Chapter Twenty-Two

Charlotte knocked on Chief Mitchell's door.

Please let this go well...

"Come in!"

She stuck her head inside. "Hey, you got a minute?"

"I do. But make it quick. The digital forensics guys are coming in to beg for updated tools and software. I've been avoiding them for weeks because I have yet to figure out how to work it into the budget."

"Don't worry. This won't take long."

Charlotte almost fell into a chair as a rush of nausea hit her square in the gut. She didn't know if it was the pregnancy, the fact that she'd let Miles talk her into sharing the news with the chief or the stench of old coffee wafting through the office.

Maybe it's a combination of all three, she thought, eyeballing several paper cups scattered along the desk.

"Any updates on the investigation?" he asked.

"Nothing that I haven't already reported. I'm actually here to discuss something else with you. But before I do, I'd like to ask that you keep it between us. At least for the time being."

"Your secret's safe with me. What's going on?"

*Just say it. And hope that he doesn't ask a bunch of
questions. Like who's the father.*

"Chief, I, um… I'm pregnant—"

Crack!

Charlotte stopped abruptly when the sound of breaking glass smashed against the door.

"What the hell was that?" Chief Mitchell yelled.

"Sorry, sir!"

Charlotte rushed to the door and threw it open. Walter was crouched down on his knees, picking up pieces
of a shattered coffee mug.

"What are you doing?" she hissed.

He looked up at her, his eyes red with anger. "Just
trying to get to my desk. I must've slipped on something and dropped my cup in the process."

"Right outside of Chief Mitchell's office, huh? Just
as I'd come in here to have a private conversation. How
coincidental." She crossed her arms in front of her chest
and leaned against the doorway. "Maybe you got tripped
up after overhearing my conversation. Were you standing out here eavesdropping on us?"

"*Eavesdropping?* Why would I care about whatever
it is you two are talking about?"

"Oh, please. Let's not act like you haven't been overly
concerned with every move I make since my promotion. Not to mention our failed—"

Charlotte stopped herself.

"Not to mention our failed *what*?" Walter asked,
standing straight up as a crowd began to gather. "Our
failed relationship? You sound a bit paranoid, Bowman.
Could it be that those threats you *allegedly* keep get-

ting are throwing you off? Or maybe it's the fact that you have yet to solve this case."

An audible gasp rippled through the area. Charlotte ignored the instigators, focusing solely on Walter while fighting the urge to punch him in the throat.

"Walk away, Corporal Kincaid," she warned.

Instead of taking heed, he moved in closer. "Or maybe you're finally realizing that you're in too deep, thanks to that premature promotion, *Sarge*."

"Go to hell, Walter—"

"Hey!" Chief Mitchell barked just as the digital forensics team walked up.

"You ready for us, Chief?" the director asked.

"Yeah, come on in, guys. Sergeant Bowman, let's reconvene later this afternoon. And, Corporal Kincaid? Watch it. That's a superior you're talking to."

"Yes, sir," Walter said, his exaggerated tone far from sincere.

Charlotte slipped past everyone and hurried toward her office. She grabbed the door to slam it shut. A hand forced it back open. She pivoted, almost slamming into Miles.

"Hey, you okay?" he asked.

"No, not really." She grabbed a tissue and patted the back of her damp neck. "I was just in Chief Mitchell's office, sharing the news that I'm pregnant. Walter was loitering right outside the door. I think he may have overheard our conversation."

"Wait, I ran out to the parking lot for five minutes and missed all of that? Let me go and have a word with Walter—"

"No!" Charlotte insisted, pulling him back inside the

office. "Walter is already questioning my capabilities as a sergeant. I don't want him thinking I can't fight my own battles, too. I appreciate the gesture, though."

"Of course. That's what I'm here for. Don't worry about that clown. You've got way bigger things to think about. So, how did Chief Mitchell react to the news?"

"He didn't get a chance to. As soon as the words *I'm pregnant* were out of my mouth, Walter smashed a mug right outside of the office. Then the digital forensics guys came in for a meeting. It was just chaotic. The chief and I are going to reconvene later this afternoon."

"Okay, well, at least he's aware of what's going on. Now, grab your purse. I've got a surprise for you."

"A surprise? What kind of surprise?"

"The kind you'll find out about in fifteen minutes. Let's go!"

"Um, I don't mean to burst your bubble or anything," Charlotte said when Miles pulled in front of the Drip & Sip Coffee Shop, "but coming to this place is not a surprise."

"Woman, just get out of the car and follow me."

The scent of frosted cinnamon rolls hit well before they entered the café. Charlotte clutched her grumbling stomach.

"On second thought, maybe this little coffee run is exactly what I needed."

"Trust me," Miles said, holding open the door, "it is."

"Charlotte!" someone screamed the moment they stepped inside. She swiveled and almost tipped over at the sight of Ella charging toward her.

"El! What are you doing here?"

"I was just assigned another temp job in Reno. So of course I had to stop through River Valley again and see my big sis on the way there."

"Aww, I'm so glad you did." Charlotte squeezed her watery eyes shut as she embraced her sister. "Miles was right. I did need this surprise, and he seems to always know where to find you. There's been so much going on. The stress of this investigation has taken over my entire life."

"Don't let it. You've got my little niece or nephew to think about," Ella insisted now that Charlotte and Miles had shared the pregnancy news with their immediate families.

"That's exactly what I've been telling her," Miles said.

"I'm working on it." Charlotte glanced around the quaint shop, eyeing its long rustic tables, antique bookshelves and old album covers hanging from the walls.

"I love this place," Ella gushed. "Nice choice, Miles. I found an empty table near the back by the window for us."

"Cool," he said. "Why don't you two have a seat and I'll place our order? Charlotte, should I get your regular? A decaf caramel macchiato and cinnamon roll?"

"*Two* cinnamon rolls. Don't judge me."

"Never would I do that. Ella, what are you having?"

"I'd like a mocha latte and everything bagel, please."

"Got it. Be right back."

Ella clutched Charlotte's hand and led her to their table. "Okay, so, how wonderful is Miles?"

"He's… Yeah. He's a great guy."

"Uh-oh."

"Uh-oh, what?"

"I know that tone. It's the same one you had back when you first met Miles, then dumped him after three days of pure bliss!"

"You are so dramatic. That is not how it happened."

"That's exactly how it happened. And now, I already know you're about to go into the whole *I'm going through too much to even think about a relationship* spiel. Only this time, the excuse will be your case rather than the divorce, which was your excuse the last time."

"I hate that I share everything with you." Charlotte stared down at the table, running her nails along its rigid grooves. "Look, it's not that simple. I've already explained to Miles that this case is my number one priority. I can't get distracted by a relationship right now."

"Seriously?" Ella pointed at her belly. "Seems like you're already past that point. You and Miles are in each other's lives permanently now. Plus, it's not all about you anymore. That man dropped his entire life back in California to be here for you. That says a lot. And he's so excited about becoming a father. Shoot, I wish I could find a distraction that wonderful."

Clanking dishes rattled behind Charlotte. "Look, he's on his way back here. Let's table this conversation for later. Better yet, let's just drop it altogether."

"Whatever you say…"

Miles approached balancing a tray and his cell phone. "You're looking good, big bro," he said to the screen. "You been hitting the gym behind my back?"

"No doubt," Miles's brother, Jake, replied, flexing his biceps.

Charlotte passed their drinks around and leaned into the phone. "Hey, Jake. How are you?"

"Hey, I'm hanging in there. How are things going out there in the desert? Any new leads on the case?"

"Things are moving. We've got a few interesting bites we're looking into."

"Who is that?" Ella whispered.

"My brother," Miles told her.

"Who is that?" Jake asked.

"My sister, Ella," Charlotte said.

Miles turned the phone in Ella's direction.

"Damn!" Jake uttered. "Oh, wait, sorry. I shouldn't have— I was just…"

"Taken aback by my sister's beauty?" Charlotte finished for him.

"Yeah, actually. I was. Let me check my schedule real quick and see when I can take a trip to River Valley. You know, to check on my baby brother. See if he needs a little of my Clemmington PD expertise."

"Oh, so you work in law enforcement, too?" Ella asked.

"I do. I'm a detective."

"Mmm, interesting. It just so happens that I love a man in uniform."

Charlotte side-eyed her sister, then tapped Miles's arm. "Sorry Ella hijacked your video chat," she whispered.

"No worries. It's actually nice to see Jake vibing with someone. His dating life hasn't been the smoothest, to say the least."

"Listen, guys," Jake said, "I need to get going. Duty calls. Miles and Charlotte, let me know if there's anything I can do to help out on my end. And I mean that. The investigation, the pregnancy, whatever."

"Thanks, man," Miles said. "We appreciate it."

"And, Ella," Jake continued, his voice dropping several octaves, "it was a pleasure meeting you, albeit digitally. Hopefully next time we can do so in person."

She flipped her hair and flashed a red-carpet smile. "Yes, that would be nice."

The pair grew silent while gazing at one another through the screen.

"Bye, Jake," Charlotte interjected.

Miles disconnected the chat and took a sip of his chai tea. "So, what'd I miss? I saw you two sitting back here gossiping while I was up at the counter."

"Who, *us*?" Charlotte glanced around the café in mock confusion. "Gossiping? Why, we'd never…"

"Actually," Ella cut in, "we were talking about how wonderful you are, and how I am so looking forward to being an auntie."

"Aww, thanks. But not as much as I'm looking forward to being a dad."

"Sweet." A line of worry suddenly creased Ella's forehead. "Speaking of parenthood, Charlotte, I'm assuming you're going to back off this investigation and focus on your pregnancy now, right?"

Charlotte picked up a napkin and fanned her face as the air in the room grew warmer. She could feel Miles's eyes on her, awaiting her response.

"Listen," she began, "I know how much you both care about me. And I appreciate it. But I'm committed to seeing this case through to the end. Nothing either of you say is going to change that. Plus, I'm healthy, the baby is healthy and the doctor hasn't mentioned anything about me needing to dial it back. So don't worry. I'll be fine. *We'll* be fine."

"I hope you're not doing this because you think you have something to prove," Miles said.

"Not at all. Proof of my abilities was validated when Chief Mitchell promoted me over everyone else in the department. Now, am I bothered by the fact that I have yet to solve this investigation? Absolutely. Is the media pressure getting to me? Definitely."

"See," Ella said, shaking her head so hard that her curls slapped against her face. "I don't like that. You're stressing yourself out, Char. Listen to me. I'm a nurse. You're gonna end up jeopardizing yourself *and* the baby over this case. You've got to take into consideration what all that pressure could do to your body. There's the threat of gestational diabetes, preeclampsia and premature birth, just to name a few."

The fanning of the napkin was no longer working. Charlotte had broken out into a full-blown sweat. "But imagine the amount of stress I'd be under if I let this case go. Some of my colleagues are waiting on me to fail. So much so that one of them has been threatening me to try and throw me off."

"We don't know that for a fact," Miles said.

"Well, what we do know for a fact is there are people in that department who resent me."

"And by people," Ella said, "do you mean Walter?"

"Not just Walter. But he's certainly number one on my list."

Ella brushed a few flyaways out of Charlotte's eyes. "I'm getting the sense that you're irritated."

"That's because I am. And I'd love to change the subject. A surprise visit from my sister is supposed to be enjoyable. I'm not enjoying this tag-teaming interrogation you two are putting me through."

"You're right," Ella said just as the bell over the shop's door jingled. A commotion erupted near the entrance.

"Stephanie!" a male voice boomed. "How's the owner of my favorite coffee spot in town doing?"

Charlotte groaned, immediately recognizing that loud, irritating voice. "What in the hell is Walter doing here? Do you think he followed us?"

"I certainly hope not," Miles responded. "But if he did, it wouldn't surprise me. Either way, don't worry about it. Just relax and enjoy your coffee and cinnamon rolls."

"I've suddenly lost my appetite."

"Oh, no," Ella said, sliding the plate toward her. "Eat up. Don't allow that man to get to you. Let him see you back here having a good time."

Charlotte stared at the rolls. Buttercream icing oozed down the sides of the warm pastries. "You're right. What was I thinking?"

The moment she bit into the gooey dessert, Walter came strolling over.

"Hey, what's up, everybody? Did my invite to this little shindig get lost in the mail or something?"

"Hello," Ella grumbled while Miles and Charlotte ignored him.

"I just so happened to be driving by and saw you three sitting in the window. So I figured I'd come in and say hello. Especially to you, Ella. It's been a long time. How've you been?"

Ella glared up at him, her lips twisted with disgust. "Wonderful. Especially after hearing the news that Charlotte and Miles are expecting—"

Charlotte gave her a swift kick underneath the table. "*Ouch!* What was that... *Ohh.*"

"Wait," Walter said. "Expecting what? Go on and finish what you were saying, Ella. Charlotte and Miles are expecting..."

A ringing cell phone disrupted the moment.

"*Thank* you," Charlotte whispered, ecstatic for the disruption.

Ella scrambled for her phone and turned away from the group.

"So, what news is your sister referring to?" Walter pressed.

"Charlotte and I are anticipating a visit to Reno once Ella starts her next temp job there," Miles told him.

"Really?" Walter questioned, his smirk reeking of skepticism. "Are you sure that's what it is?"

"Positive," Charlotte shot back.

Ella grabbed her things, interrupting the debate. "Sorry to break up the party. But that was the hospital administrator. I need to get to Reno. Stat." She hugged Charlotte and Miles. "So good seeing you two. Char, I'll call you later tonight."

"Better yet, text me and let me know you made it!" she called out as Ella rushed toward the exit.

"Hey, wait up!" Walter ran after her, bumping into several chairs along the way. "I'll walk you to your car!"

"Look who's trying to be a gentleman," Miles said.

"Please. More like he's trying to pry information out of her. That was a close call."

"Sure was. You shut Ella down just in time."

Charlotte drained her cup and wrapped a half-eaten cinnamon roll in a napkin. "Miles, I really appreciate you setting this up. Thank you."

"Of course."

"Why don't we head back to the station? I wanna take another look at the surveillance footage from The Bottomless Bar. See if we can figure out where Stephen could've ended up. Afterward, maybe we can drive over to Rush Street and retrace his steps."

Miles remained quiet while piling their dishes onto the tray.

"You know," Charlotte continued, "let's walk that backstreet near Eden's Den, just to see what we might find."

Still nothing. She studied his somber expression as he stood, then followed him out of the shop. When they reached the car, he stopped her.

"May I make a suggestion?" Miles asked.

"Sure."

"Why don't we review the surveillance footage at the station and have Officer Haney walk the area?"

"I know what you're doing," Charlotte retorted. "And it's not gonna work."

"Think of it this way. If you start passing some of the caseload on to other officers, whoever's threatening you may back off, and—"

"That's not gonna happen." She flung open the car door and climbed inside. "So just drop it."

He stood there, gripping the door frame. Charlotte stared straight ahead, her stony expression unflinching. "Okay, then. Consider it dropped."

Chapter Twenty-Three

Charlotte knocked on the guest room door. There was no answer. She stuck her head inside. Miles was lying across the bed sound asleep, the remote still in his hand.

She glanced at the clock. It was a little after 8:00 p.m.

Just don't wake up within the next hour, she thought before grabbing her purse and tiptoeing out the front door.

Charlotte hurried inside the car and headed straight to Rush Street. Miles had refused to take her earlier that afternoon, insisting that she needed to dial it back. While he may have won that battle, he hadn't won the war. Because now that he was out cold, she was determined to press on toward the goal of gathering new evidence with or without him.

She made a right turn down Cottonwood Lane. The narrow, two-lane street was surrounded by a nature preserve, filled with diverse flora and fauna. Charlotte switched on the bright lights as darkness enveloped her car.

Anxious to get to the other side of the preserve, she rammed her foot against the accelerator. She hadn't been out driving alone in quite some time. It evoked an eerie sense of vulnerability. She'd taken for granted the comfort of Miles's presence as memories of the Peak Avenue car chase flashed through her mind.

Turn around. Go back home. You promised, no more solo missions...

But Charlotte refused. She was feeling defiant after the confrontation with Miles outside of the coffee shop. She didn't need to prove to him she was still capable even while pregnant. She felt the need to prove it to herself. At this point, her determination trumped all sensibility. Backing down wasn't an option.

"You should at least call him," she muttered to herself. "So he'll know where you are. *Somebody* should."

Charlotte tapped the phone button on the car's touch screen.

"Miles Love."

His name appeared in the contacts list. She reached out. Her fingertip hovered over the selection. As she contemplated placing the call—

Bam!

Charlotte's head snapped back, slamming against the headrest. The car jolted forward before careening into a ditch and burrowing in the shoulder of the roadway.

Brakes screeched behind her. Bright lights shone through the back windshield, illuminating the interior of the car. Charlotte peered through the window, struggling to blink through the dizziness and adjust her blurred vision.

This cannot be happening...

"Ma'am!" a high-pitched voice called out. "I am so sorry! Are you okay?"

Relief hit when Charlotte realized she'd been rear-ended by a woman rather than the killer. She rolled her window all the way down. "I'm fine. I think. My head is a little woozy, but other than that, I'm good."

"Looks like I did a number on your car's bumper," the driver said, keeping her distance as she surveyed the damage. "Mine, too. I should not have come out here..."

"What do you mean?" Charlotte asked.

"I recently had a retinal detachment surgery. Guess I should've waited a little longer before getting back behind the wheel."

Charlotte climbed out of the car and stumbled, falling against the door.

"Oh, no! Are you sure you're all right?"

"I am. Just trying to steady my legs. They're a little wobbly." She continued toward the back of the car. "Whoa. You're right. You did do a number on my bumper. The left side is completely hanging off."

The woman covered her mouth, whimpering into her palm. "Ooh, I am so, so sorry. Let me grab my insurance info. They'll take care of everything."

Charlotte watched as the driver jogged toward her car. Her vision was still hazy, but she was able to make out a black baseball cap and oversize black windbreaker.

Several moments passed before the woman stepped back out of her car. She switched off the headlights, then slowly approached. Charlotte tried to get a better look at her face but couldn't see well through the darkness.

"Here you go," the driver said, handing her a piece of paper.

Charlotte looked down at her hands. They were hidden beneath motorcycle gloves.

"Again, my apologies."

The voice sounded a bit deeper this time.

Or are you just hearing things because you're out of it?

Charlotte's skin prickled with alarm. Something wasn't right.

"Thank you," she said, taking the paper with one hand while reaching into her waistband with the other. It came up empty. Her gun must've slipped out when she was hit.

"You're welcome, Sergeant Bowman."

Run!

Charlotte pivoted, charging toward her car. Hot, sticky leather scraped against the back of her neck. The driver grabbed her by the collar and knocked her to the ground.

"Time to finish what I started!"

The voice now resembled the attacker who'd broken into her house.

"No!" Charlotte screamed, the soles of her sneakers digging into the dry dirt as he dragged her into the preserve. "Let me go!"

He flung her body against a tree trunk. She moaned, sliding to the ground as bark tore through her shirt. Charlotte clutched her back while struggling to her knees.

A pair of headlights shone in the distance.

"Help!" she screamed, praying someone would hear her. *"Help!"*

The car got closer. Beams of light flickered through the trees. Charlotte caught a glimpse of her attacker pulling a syringe from his pocket. She kicked her foot in the air, desperate to knock it from his hand.

"Stand down!" he yelled, grabbing her leg and pulling until she fell backward.

Charlotte screamed, her head pounding the hard soil as she bit down on her tongue. The taste of metal filled her mouth.

Get up. Don't you give in. Get up and fight!

She pulled herself onto her elbows, expelling a chunk of blood before wiping dirt from her eyes. When her vision cleared, she watched in horror as the assailant raised his foot high in the air. A heavy black boot hovered over her stomach.

My baby! a voice screeched inside of her head.

And then...

Boom!

"Ahhh!"

The man yelled out in pain after his foot slammed against a stone buried beneath the dirt. Charlotte had managed to roll over seconds before his boot made contact. She flinched at the sound of his cracking bones.

He lost his balance, stumbling backward. Charlotte kicked her foot high in the air. The firm tip of her shoe landed right between his legs. His animalistic howl reverberated through the preserve as he toppled over in agony.

"You bitch!"

Charlotte hobbled to her feet and bolted toward the car.

"Do *not* let him get away this time!" she cried out, throwing open the door and frantically searching for her gun.

Got it.

Charlotte stumbled back into the preserve. She

pushed her way through branches, desperate to find her attacker.

A dark shadow whizzed by in the distance.

Pop! Pop!

She fired a couple of shots. They ricocheted off a tree truck and disappeared into the distance.

Keep going!

Charlotte made her way toward the area where the assailant had lain clutching his groin. He was gone.

No, no, no!

"Where the hell are you?" she yelled.

Silence.

She ran to the left, then right. There was no sign of him anywhere.

An engine roared from the road. Charlotte hurried back toward the street. When she reached the area where their cars had been parked, hers was the only one there.

"He's gone," she sobbed, spinning in circles as tears burned her eyes. "I cannot believe this. He's gone!"

Charlotte stared down Cottonwood Lane. Taillights flickered in the far distance. She jumped inside her car and sped toward the vehicle. But after driving over two miles, she realized that it was too late. Her attacker had gotten away once again.

"Nooo!" she screamed, banging her fist against the dashboard.

Charlotte's fingers shook as she jabbed the phone button on the touch screen and hit Miles's name. He picked up on the first ring.

"Hey, where are you?" he asked. "I didn't know you left the house. I've been calling you—"

"I messed up, Miles. Bad. Really bad."

"What do you mean? What happened?"

"I was attacked!"

"*What?* When?"

"Just a few minutes ago. I was heading to Rush Street and got rear-ended on Cottonwood Lane. When I got out to check the damage on my car, the driver attacked me. It was the killer, Miles. I was able to fight him off, but I almost died!"

Charlotte heard a car door slam through the phone.

"Are you still on Cottonwood Lane?" he panted.

"Yes. But I'm on my way to the police station. Just meet me there."

"No! I want you to go straight to the hospital. You and the baby need to get checked out before we do anything else."

"But I'm okay, Miles. *We're* fine."

"This is not up for debate, Charlotte. You have got to see a doctor, just to be safe. You're not a superhero, contrary to what you seem to believe. Something might be wrong and you just don't know it yet."

The road ahead blurred as Charlotte's eyes filled with tears. "Okay. I'll head to River Valley Memorial now. If nothing else, I think I need stitches in my tongue."

"You what?"

"I'll tell you about it later."

"All right. I'll call Chief Mitchell and let him know what happened. Were you able to get a look at the suspect or his vehicle this time?"

"Not really, no. It was so dark, and I was completely disoriented after he crashed into me. Plus, in all honesty, I had my guard down. At first, I thought it was a woman—"

Charlotte paused.

"Hello?" Miles said.

"I'm here. Something just dawned on me. When I was being attacked, the killer seemed to be laser focused on my stomach. He tried to stomp me right in the middle of it. Why would he do that? Of all the areas on my body, why was he concentrating on my stomach?"

"I think I know where you're going with this. Walter overheard you telling Chief Mitchell that you're pregnant, and he's the one who's behind the assault?"

"Exactly!"

"But wouldn't you have known if it was Walter who attacked you?"

"My car had just been hit, Miles. *Hard.* I was completely disoriented and could barely see through the darkness."

His throaty sigh whooshed through the car speakers. "Maybe it's time for you to discuss your suspicions about him with Chief Mitchell. And we should find out where he was tonight. See if he can be accounted for."

"I totally agree. It's long overdue…" Charlotte's voice faded. She'd managed to cheat death yet again, at the hands of someone she was once so close to. "Hey, can you stay on the phone with me until I get to the hospital?"

"You don't even have to ask."

Chapter Twenty-Four

Charlotte sat on Ella's couch, holding her sister as she wept in her lap.

It had been three days since Charlotte's attack. After much resistance, Miles and Chief Mitchell were able to talk her into taking a break, at least for a short period. The chief was adamant that she do so considering the pregnancy. His wife even called to express her concern.

The pain of stepping away hurt Charlotte worse than the actual assault. But she needed the time to recover as they awaited Chief Mitchell's response to their findings on Walter.

That evening, she and Miles had been sitting out on the deck relaxing when Ella called. They'd assumed she was reaching out to check on Charlotte. But the terror in her voice said otherwise.

"Somebody tried to kill me!" she'd screamed into the phone.

Within minutes, Charlotte and Miles were inside the car, heading to Reno. And now, as he spoke quietly with police near the doorway, Charlotte struggled to comfort her inconsolable sister.

"I cannot believe this happened to me," Ella whimpered.

Charlotte's jaw tightened as anger burned through her body. "Neither can I. I should've had that man locked up a long time ago. I am so sorry, El." She studied the red strangulation marks lining Ella's throat and the small scar sliced into her left cheek.

"I'm so glad you were able to get away from that maniac before he was able to do any more damage. But I really wish you would've gone to the hospital. You have got to stop being so hardheaded."

"For the tenth time," Ella argued, "I feel safer here at the apartment rather than some wide-open, public place. Victims are the most vulnerable inside of hospitals."

"Yeah, maybe in the movies. But not in real life."

"Okay, everyone," one of the policemen said. "We're gonna join the other officers down in the parking lot who are examining the scene. Let us know if you need anything, or if Ella remembers something that's not already in the report."

"Will do," Miles said. "Thank you." He closed the door and took a seat on the arm of the couch. "How are you feeling, El?"

"Sore. And pissed off. But I'll be all right."

"She's finally calming down," Charlotte whispered.

Miles nodded. "Aside from Charlotte, do you realize that you're the first victim who's managed to get away from the killer?"

"I do. I fought him off like my life depended on it, because it did. That man sliced at my face, and I saw a syringe almost fall from his pocket. Who knows what was inside of it."

"That's what we're trying to figure out," Charlotte said. "What could this man be using to kill his victims?"

Miles pulled out his notebook. "Ella, I know you've been through a lot and you're probably still in shock. But do you feel up to telling us exactly what happened, from the time you left work to the time you were assaulted?"

"I do," she moaned, slowly sitting up. "I wanna do whatever I can to help end this nightmare."

"Can I get you anything before you start?" Charlotte asked. "Water? Tea? Something stronger?"

"I'd love something stronger. But I've got to be in my right mind when I tell this story. So no, thanks."

Miles tapped his pen against the pad. "Ready when you are."

Ella took in a deep breath of air. "Okay, so I left work a little after seven o'clock. I stopped at Dickerson's and picked up a salad on the way home. It was going on eight o'clock by the time I pulled into the apartment complex. I parked my car, and right before I reached the stairwell, somebody snatched me up and dragged me into the wooded area behind the complex."

"Did you get a look at the guy?" Miles asked.

"Not really. He was dressed in all black and wearing a ski mask."

"What about his height and size?"

Ella wiped her eyes, smearing navy blue eyeliner across her cheeks. "It's all a blur, really. I was so flustered. And of course terrified. From what I could see, he was pretty tall. Definitely over six feet. And his clothes were baggy. But if I had to guess, he appeared more on the slim side."

Miles took rigorous notes before glancing over at Charlotte. "Sounds like the description you gave of your attacker."

"I definitely think it's the same per-person." Her voice cracked. She wanted to be strong for Miles, and especially for Ella. But she was beginning to unravel under the weight of the situation.

"Okay," Miles continued, "so your attacker was tall, thin, dressed in all black and wearing a ski mask. Did you get a look at his eyes?"

"No. Not really. I just remember seeing two dark, evil slits."

"So dark eyes, possibly."

Ella coughed, then cringed while clutching her throat.

"You need some hot tea," Charlotte told her.

"Hot tea? I need some drugs. Can you grab the bottle of oxycodone out of my purse?"

"Didn't you just take an oxy about thirty minutes ago?"

"Look," Ella said, rolling off the couch and limping toward the kitchen counter, "I took one over an hour ago. Did you forget that I'm a nurse? I know what I'm doing. I promise you, I will not overdose or become addicted."

Charlotte rolled her eyes and looked to Miles for backup.

"She's been through a lot," he whispered. "Just let her be."

Charlotte nodded and walked over to the window. "Looks like there are several more squad cars down in the lot. And dozens of officers examining that wooded area."

Ella came back into the living room carrying a piece of paper. "Do you all want to see the police report?"

"Definitely," Miles said while Charlotte rejoined him. As they skimmed the report, Ella let out a loud groan.

Charlotte sprang from the couch. "What's wrong?"

"I missed three calls from my boss. She is freaking out on my voice mail. Word must be getting around about the attack. I'm gonna go call her back. Can you give me a few minutes?"

"Of course. Take your time."

The second she was out of the room, Charlotte collapsed onto Miles's shoulder.

"I cannot believe what I'm reading," she whimpered, the police report shaking in her hand. "My sister was *brutally* assaulted. Dragged, kicked, strangled, cut..."

Her voice trailed off as the soft cry turned into a full-blown sob. Miles wrapped his arm around her. "But you know what? Ella survived. To the point where she's turned down medical attention. The woman is tough. And so are you. Keep pushing. We've come too far in this investigation to let it get the best of us now."

"I won't..."

Charlotte's cell phone buzzed. It was a text from Chief Mitchell.

Anybody seen or heard from Corporal Kincaid? He's been MIA since this morning. If anyone knows of his whereabouts, let me know ASAP!

"Miles!" she hissed, handing him the phone. "Look at this."

He scanned the message, then propped his head in his hand. "My God..."

"That psychopath has been in Reno all day, stalking Ella so he could attack her! But listen, don't say anything to her about this just yet. I want Ella to focus on recovering—"

She stopped abruptly when Ella walked back in.

"My boss is so sweet. She offered to come and stay the night with me so I wouldn't be alone."

"But I was going to stay with you," Charlotte told her.

"You don't have to do that. I'll be fine. Plus, you need to get back to River Valley. You *are* the sergeant, after all. And don't you two wanna hit the streets and find the monster who did this to me?"

"Absolutely," Miles affirmed. "That's our number one priority. That, and making sure you're okay."

When Ella sat back down on the couch, Charlotte stared at the bandage covering her cheek. Thoughts of torturing Walter, then shooting him dead crossed her mind.

"I wish I could thank that group of teenagers who pulled into the parking lot blaring their music," Ella said. "I think that's what threw off my attacker. He didn't drag me far enough into the wooded area for us to totally go unseen, because I was fighting too hard."

"My girl," Charlotte said, giving her hand a squeeze.

Ella jumped when the doorbell rang.

"You're okay," Miles told her. "That's probably your boss, isn't it?"

"Ugh. It's gonna take me a minute to work through this PTSD."

As Ella headed to the door, Charlotte leaned toward Miles and whispered, "I'm texting Chief Mitchell right now, letting him know that I think Walter is behind Ella's attack. I'll wait until we leave to call him. I don't want her to hear the conversation and get more upset than she already is."

"Good. While you do that, I'll take screenshots of the police report so we'll have a copy of it."

Ella stood in the living room's entryway embracing a short, chubby redhead who looked to be in her early sixties.

"You know you didn't have to come over," she told her.

"Don't be ridiculous, sweetheart. I had to make sure you were okay. Plus, being here with you means I can enjoy a night away from my snoring husband. *And*," she continued, holding up a plastic bag, "I bought snacks on the way here that I'm not supposed to be eating. Chocolate, Cheetos, Chex Mix…"

Charlotte and Miles stood when Ella walked her boss into the room.

"Patrice, this is my sister, Sergeant Charlotte Bowman, and her partner, Detective Miles Love. They're investigating the Numeric Serial Killer case."

"Nice to meet you both," Patrice said, bypassing their extended hands in exchange for hugs. "Thank you for your service. And don't worry. I'll keep a close watch on the place tonight." She nudged Ella's arm and patted her purse. "I packed my…you know…just in case—"

"*Okay*," Ella interrupted. "Char, Miles, why don't you two head back. I know you've got a lot of work ahead of you."

"Are you sure you'll be okay without us here?" Charlotte asked.

"Positive. I've got Patrice with me, and the cops have the place under surveillance."

Patrice held her handbag in the air and gave the group a wink. "Don't forget what's in here!"

"And on that note," Ella said, walking Charlotte and Miles to the door. "Before you even ask," she whispered, "yes, Patrice has a license to carry."

"Wasn't gonna say a word," Charlotte replied. "Listen, if you need anything, *anything*, just call me and we'll turn the car right back around. Do you understand me?"

"Yes, I understand. And I thank you. But I'll be fine. Thank you for getting here so fast, and for putting me back together. Because I was in shambles when you two got here."

"Understandably so," Miles told her. "And like your sister said, if you need us, call us."

"I will. Be careful. And keep me posted."

Charlotte waited for the door to close behind her before she let the tears fall. She swiped them away, not wanting Miles to see her crying. When they reached the parking lot, she approached the police chief and gave him her card, asking that he reach out with any updates.

"Should we head straight to the station?" Miles asked on the way to the car.

"Definitely." She checked her phone. "No response from Chief Mitchell. I'll try calling him now."

Miles looked on expectantly.

"Voice mail," she told him before leaving a message. "Chief, it's Sergeant Bowman. I need for you to call me as soon as you get this message. Corporal Kincaid needs to be located and apprehended immediately. We're positive that he's behind these attacks."

She shoved the phone inside her purse and looked to Miles. "We need to get to River Valley in record time and join in on the search."

"I'll drive as fast as I can."

Right before he opened the passenger door, Charlotte noticed a flash of metal glimmering off the asphalt a couple of spaces over. "Wait," she said, pointing at the ground. "What is that?" She led Miles toward a maroon Toyota Camry. "I just spotted something near that car's left rear tire."

He turned on his cell phone's flashlight while she pulled a pair of latex gloves from her purse. "It looks like a piece of jewelry or something."

Charlotte picked up the piece and held it under the light, studying the steel link bracelet. "It's a watch." She dusted off the sapphire-blue dial, then turned it over. "And it's engraved."

"Can you make out the lettering?"

"I think so." She pulled it closer, squinting while trying to read the tiny inscription. "Hold on. Let me scrape the dust off the back. It says, *W, J…* WJK."

"WJK," Miles repeated. "That could be anybody. Let's send it to the lab and have the fingerprints lifted. You never know who—"

"Hold on!" Charlotte steadied herself against the car after almost losing her balance.

"What's wrong?"

"Those initials," she said, her skin growing cold. "They're Walter's. *Walter Jacobs Kincaid.*"

Chapter Twenty-Five

Charlotte stared out the window at the long stretch of desert road.

"I am absolutely spent. Mentally, physically, emotionally…"

Miles covered her hand with his. "I know you are. Hang in there. We're almost at the finish line."

"I wonder why Chief Mitchell hasn't gotten back to us yet."

"Why don't you try him again? And maybe suggest that he publicly name Walter a person of interest."

"I like that idea—"

A sharp pang hit Charlotte's stomach when she reached down into her purse. She placed her hand over her belly, taking in several sharp breaths until it subsided.

"You good?"

"I'm fine," she lied, not wanting him to worry. "Just trying to get to my phone." Charlotte unlocked the screen. "Wait, how did I miss three calls from the chief? I didn't even hear my phone ring." Just as she tapped his name in the Contacts list, a notification popped up.

"Now he's texting me."

"What's he saying?"

Get to the Creosote River, now! Walter's body was found washed up along the shore!

Her phone slipped out of her hand.

"Charlotte? What's going on?"

"Change of plans. Head to the Creosote River. Walter is dead."

"Walter is *what*?"

"Dead!"

She jerked back in her seat when Miles slammed down on the gas. Bile burned the back of her throat. Charlotte inhaled a rush of air, forcing it back down while searching the floor for her phone. Soon as she found it, she dialed Chief Mitchell. He picked up on the first ring.

"Please tell me you're on your way here," he choked out.

She winced at the pain in his voice. It conjured a deep level of culpability. She'd been adamant of Walter's guilt. So adamant that she had overlooked the real killer. Now Walter was dead. Ella had almost died. *She'd* almost died on more than one occasion. And a slew of other innocent victims lay dead in her wake.

"Yes, Chief," Charlotte whispered into the phone. "We're on the road now. And I am so sorry. For all of this."

"Don't be. You've just been doing your job."

She switched the call to speakerphone. "What condition was Walter's body in when he was found?"

Chief Mitchell went silent as the crime scene chaos rang out in the background.

"Are you still there?" she asked.

"I'm here. Walter's, uh—his body was in pretty good

condition, just like the other victims. And the...the number one was carved into his right cheek."

Charlotte doubled over, her head falling between her knees.

"The number one," Miles said, reaching over and gently rubbing her back. "Meaning he was killed today."

"That's what I'm assuming," the chief said. "And... that's not all."

Charlotte slowly rose up and rolled down the window. "What else?"

"There was a heart-shaped symbol carved into his chest."

"Oh, my God," she moaned. The sick feeling pooling inside her stomach intensified.

"Listen," Chief Mitchell said. "I need to go. Forensics is calling me back over. Thanks for the update on Ella. Glad she's okay. You two just get here as soon as you can."

"We will, Chief."

Charlotte glanced over at Miles. He appeared ashen, his expression immobile.

"This is unreal," he said. "The killer carved a heart into Walter's chest? He is doing everything in his power to break us."

"But it's not gonna work," she countered, feeling a second wind coming on."

Miles entered the Creosote River into the navigation system, then increased his speed along Interstate 50's desolate roadway.

Charlotte gripped the dashboard. Unsettling tremors crawled along her skin as she stared up ahead, then in the side-view mirror. They were surrounded by sand

and tumbleweed. Aside from a pair of headlights in the far distance, there were no other cars in sight. "I guess they don't call this highway the loneliest road in America for nothing."

"It is pretty damn eerie out here."

The pair grew silent for several minutes before Charlotte spoke up.

"I cannot believe Walter is dead. Why would the killer murder him?" She pressed her fingertips into her temples. "Wait, what am I saying? I know why. He's sending me a message by targeting everyone around me."

"And what do you think that message is?"

"That I'm next." Charlotte shivered at the sound of those words. "This case has taken us back to square one over and over again. But this time? We're a good ten steps behind square one."

Her cell phone buzzed. A notification from an unknown number appeared.

"Here we go." She held up the screen. "A text from an anonymous sender." Her thumb trembled as she swiped open the message.

ARE YOU READY TO DIE, SERGEANT BOWMAN? BECAUSE IT'S YOUR TURN NOW!

She gagged when a video of Walter's dead, naked body began to play. He'd been propped up on a pile of rough stones. Blood poured from the scar etched into his cheek. The top half of the heart carved into his chest was pointed, resembling a devil's horns. A zigzag line was sliced down the middle, as if it were broken. Sinister laughter could be heard in the background.

"What the hell is that?" Miles asked.

Charlotte shoved the phone into his chest. "I think I'm gonna be sick!"

He glanced at the screen before quickly turning away. "We don't need to see that. Just turn it off. We'll deal with the crime scene once we get there."

A pair of headlights flashed behind them. Charlotte jumped when a horn blared so loudly that it rattled the car.

"Why would some jerk be riding our bumper like that?" Miles asked.

She stared out of the back windshield. "I don't know. It looks like an eighteen-wheeler. I should flash my badge and tell him to pull over."

"I would under normal circumstances. But we've got a bigger situation to deal with."

The truck's horn roared once again, piercing Charlotte's ears.

Miles veered to the side of the road. "That almost blew out my eardrums!"

"Just let him pass us. He's obviously in a hurry. Maybe he's late on a delivery."

Miles let up on the accelerator and rode the shoulder. Instead of going around them, the truck slowed down while continuing to ride their bumper.

"*What* is he doing now? Didn't I give him enough room to go around us?"

"More than enough. Forget about it. He lost his chance. Let's keep going."

Miles got back on the road and sped up. Just as he drove a safe distance away, the trucker turned on his high beams and flew toward them.

"Now I can't see, and he's riding our bumper aga—"
Boom!

The car careened into the opposite lane.

"Did he just *hit* us?" Charlotte screamed.

"Yes! He did!"

Bam!

Another hit. Charlotte's head slammed against the dashboard as Miles struggled to regain control of the vehicle. They were lucky the airbags didn't deploy.

She sat up slowly. Blood poured from her nostrils.

"Charlotte! Are you all right?" Miles snatched a stack of napkins from the glove compartment while gripping the steering wheel.

She moaned, pressing them to her nose. "He must be drunk."

"Either that or we're under attack. Whatever the case, we've got two choices. Apprehend him or get the hell away from him."

Charlotte held the napkins in one hand while grabbing hold of her gun with the other. Just as she turned in her seat…

Pow!

A bullet shot through their back windshield and struck the touch screen.

"Get down!" Miles yelled right before a second bullet hit the side of his headrest.

The steering wheel jerked from side to side. He lost control of the car. Pellets of gravel slammed against the windows as a cloud of sand enveloped the car.

Charlotte gripped the door handle, watching in horror while they sped into the desert.

The vehicle jolted over jagged rocks and hardened cacti. Dust billowed everywhere.

Suddenly, everything lit up around them. Charlotte turned around. The truck had followed them off the road.

"Shoot him!" Miles yelled.

She steadied herself, rolled down the window and pressed her arm against the door frame.

Bang!

The bullet ricocheted off the truck's side-view mirror. She shot again. This time it hit the windshield, cracking the glass.

The semi shook so violently that the trailer teetered on its right side.

"Hit him again!" Miles shouted.

Pow!

The bullet hit a tire. The truck came to a stuttering halt. Sand swirled everywhere.

"Slow down!" Charlotte instructed.

Miles spun a one-eighty and came to a stop. They watched as the eighteen-wheeler's trailer fell onto its side. Miles shined the high beams directly inside the cab. It appeared dark.

Charlotte slid to the edge of her seat, struggling to see who was behind the wheel. The driver appeared to be dressed in all black. His face was hidden behind a ski mask.

"Police!" she yelled out the window. "Step out of the truck with your hands up!"

The driver didn't budge.

Miles cracked opened his door. "You've got one more time! Get out of the vehicle with your hands in the air!"

No movement. Just silence.

"Let's double-team him," Charlotte breathed. "We'll jump out together with our guns drawn but remain behind the car doors."

Miles pulled his weapon from the middle compartment. "And if that doesn't work, we'll move in on him. You ready?"

"I'm ready."

He reached over and placed his hand over her stomach. "Be careful. And I already know what you're gonna say, but you can stay here and let me handle this alone."

"Not a chance."

"Just like I thought. Okay, then. Let's go."

The pair stepped out of the car and crouched down.

"Either step out of the truck with your hands up," Charlotte warned, "or we'll come to you. And don't get it twisted. We *will* shoot!"

The driver slowly opened the door.

"Here he comes," Miles whispered. "Stay on high alert."

"I'm on it," Charlotte confirmed, her eyes laser focused on the semi.

A Timberland boot hit the step. The driver climbed out of the cab but remained behind the door.

"Now step in front of the truck with your hands in the air!" she commanded.

He didn't move.

"Walk out with your hands up!" Miles echoed.

The driver stood stoically behind the door.

"Should we move in on him?" Charlotte whispered.

"Yes. Follow my lead. But be careful. Keep in mind he's got a gun."

Miles crept from around his door. "Since you don't wanna come to us," he called out, "we're coming to you. Don't do anything stupid or else you will pay the price."

Charlotte bent down and moved around the back of the car, joining Miles. The pair stayed low, duckwalking toward the truck with their weapons aimed at the driver.

"We're moving in—"

The attacker took off running. Miles and Charlotte went charging after him. The darkness intensified as they ran farther away from the vehicles' headlights. She followed the sound of the assailant's footsteps, then took a shot. The footsteps continued.

"Dammit!" she hissed, angry that she'd missed.

Sand swirled as they stomped along the desert floor, further impairing their vision. Miles took a shot. Their attacker went tumbling to the ground.

"Stay back!" he told Charlotte. "I'm going in!"

She activated the light on her cell phone and shined it toward the man as Miles pounced on him.

"Put your hands behind your back!" he asserted.

A scuffle ensued as the assailant thrashed about. Clouds of dust enveloped their bodies, making it impossible for Charlotte to make out either of the men.

"Miles!" she screamed.

No response. Only the sound of limbs scuffling through the gravel.

Pop! Pop! Pop!

Shots rang out. Charlotte fell to the ground.

"Miles!" she called out once again. Still no response.

Panic pulled her off the ground and sent her running toward the men. Just as she reached their feet, Charlotte heard the sound of clanking metal.

"You're under arrest," Miles choked out, spitting a mouthful of sand. He cranked open a pair of handcuffs, struggling to contain the attacker's wrists.

"Let me help you!" Charlotte insisted.

"No! Stand down!"

The moment Miles slipped a cuff onto the man's wrist, the assailant reached up and cracked him in the jaw.

Charlotte stepped forward with her gun aimed at the man's chest. "Miles, *move*!"

"No!" he moaned. "Don't shoot!"

She knew he wanted to arrest the killer, not carry him away in a body bag. So she retreated.

Miles and the assailant rolled through the sand once more, throwing blows as the detective struggled to cuff him. Charlotte's legs shivered as she looked on helplessly. She was dying to jump in and assist. But she couldn't. She had a baby to protect.

Through the sound of crunching gravel, Charlotte finally heard the handcuffs click.

"Got him!" Miles yelled. He stood, pulling their suspect to his feet.

She ran over and yanked off his ski mask, shining her light in his face.

The man smiled brightly.

Charlotte jumped back, almost falling to her knees.

"Surpriiise," he sang. "Happy to see me, Char Char?" The man leaned in with his lips puckered. Miles yanked him back.

"Wait," the detective said, "you know him?"

"Yes." Her voice trembled with shock. "I do. This is Noel. Noel Reed. Ella's ex-boyfriend."

MILES FLOORED THE gas pedal, speeding down Interstate 50 toward River Valley's police station. Noel sat smugly in the back seat with his hands cuffed behind his back.

Charlotte activated the Voice Memos app on her cell phone and began recording the conversation.

"Why, Noel?" she asked. "What would possess you to kill all those innocent people?"

He leaned on his left elbow, his head cocked as he stared at her.

"The answer to that question is simple, really. I killed them because of you."

"Because of *me*? Why?"

"*Why?* Ha! You mean to tell me you don't know?"

Miles glanced in the rearview mirror. "Stop with the BS and answer the question."

Noel scooted over as far as his seat belt would allow and looked Charlotte directly in the eyes. "The reason why I killed all those innocent people was to get back at you. You! The one who talked the only woman I ever loved into leaving me."

Charlotte felt her rapid heartbeat pulsating out of her chest. "That's what this is about? You decided to become a serial killer because Ella ended your three-month relationship?"

"Don't talk to me like our union was nothing!"

"Hey!" Miles yelled. "Keep your voice down and show some respect."

Noel's head jerked back and hit the seat when Miles slammed down on the accelerator. "Slow down, man!" He glared at Charlotte. "You should've stayed out of my effing business. Let me and Ella be happy. But *nooo*. Her lonely, single, jealous big sister just had to butt in and convince her to dump me. So I did what any sane person would do. I found a way to keep you occupied, *Sergeant Bowman*. You know, interfered with your work since I couldn't interfere with your personal life. After all, you don't have one. Well, you do now, apparently. By the way, congratulations on the pregnancy, you two!"

"How do you know about that?"

"Now, Charlotte. Did you honestly think I wouldn't hack into my lady love's email so I could keep up with her every move?"

"You are a psychopath. Not to mention a raging freak."

"No, I'm just a man who wants what he wants. And when I can't get it, I do bad things."

"Evil," Charlotte whispered. "Just pure evil."

"Wait, let me get this straight," Miles said. "You attacked, kidnapped and killed innocent people just to take Sergeant Bowman's focus off your relationship?"

"Yep." Noel smirked. "That, plus payback. But then I realized that it wasn't working. I *still* wasn't getting what I wanted. So I had to beat Ella's ass—"

"Hey!" Charlotte yelled. "Watch your mouth!"

"Oh, what are you so upset about? At least I spared her life!"

Charlotte fought the urge to grab her gun and shoot him dead, right there on the spot.

"Why did you kill Corporal Kincaid?" Miles asked.

Noel snorted. "I bet you Charlotte was happy about that one. Ella told me she couldn't stand him. I even tried to do Charlotte a favor by pinning the murders on him. Planting his watch near Ella's apartment complex was genius, wasn't it?"

"*Why* did you kill him?"

"Because I caught him trying to get with my girl!"

"What are you talking about?" Charlotte asked.

"Oh, don't act like you can't remember. That day you all were at some coffee shop. I followed Ella there. Saw Corporal Kincaid walk her out, flirting and dancing peacock in heat."

"You *completely* misread that one," Charlotte said. "They were actually arguing."

"Even worse, Sergeant! What business did he have fighting with my woman?" Noel stared out the window, his upper lip curling into a scowl. "Nothing I ever did worked. The threats and murders didn't stop Charlotte's nosy ass from meddling in our relationship. Ella didn't reach out to me after she was attacked. And I waited, too. But she called the police instead. That pissed me off so bad that I *had* to kill Walter. I was ready, too. He'd been tied up in my basement all day. But don't worry, he won't be missed. He was a douchebag. Right, Charlotte?"

She ignored him, despite his piercing eyes scrutinizing her.

"No matter how hard I tried," Noel continued, "I couldn't scare you off this case. I should've killed you when I had the chance. But I didn't. Because of Ella. Now I'm probably gonna go to prison for the rest of my life."

"*Probably?*" Miles shot back. "With six counts of first-degree murder and two counts of attempted murder? You'll definitely be locked up for life."

"So how did you do it?" Charlotte asked. "How did you kill your victims?"

Noel threw his head back and unleashed a shrill cackle. "Aww, wouldn't you like to know."

"Yes. I would."

"Let's just say I drew inspiration from some of the greats. First I injected them, like Charles Cullen, aka the Angel of Death, did to his victims. Then I carved my numeric signature into their flesh, similar to my boy Roger Flender, aka The Deity."

"You were inspired by a fictional character on a TV show?"

"Why, yes, I was. *Bones* to be exact. Good job, Char Char."

"Do not call me that."

"My apologies, Charlala. Anyway, Roger Flender's modus operandi was brilliant. That, sprinkled with a bit of Peter Ballentine's method of carving a heart into Walter's chest, and *boom*! You've got yourselves a multidimensional copycat killer who kept River Valley PD befuddled for *months*!"

The weight of remorse crushed Charlotte's chest. While she and Walter may not have been on the best of terms, and he'd made some questionable moves during the investigation, his intentions were good. He just wanted to help solve the case. In the end, it cost him his life.

"Don't you all wanna know how I put my victims out of their misery?" Noel asked, his cartoonish tone oozing with glee.

"That was my next question," Miles said.

"Welp, after I held them captive in my basement until

I got tired of looking at them, I injected them with, drumroll please, *da-da-da-da-da*…potassium chloride! Copious, copious amounts of potassium chloride. Wasn't that a brilliant choice? It's hard to detect, exits the system quickly, and most importantly? It's *deadly*. Learned all of that from the great Nurse Ella Bowman."

"So you used medication you stole from Ella to kill people?"

"No! Of course not. I may be a murderer, but I'm nobody's thief. Like I said, I learned about it from her. One day when I was digging through her medicine bag looking for aspirin, and by aspirin I mean percs, I saw a glass vial and asked what it was. She told me it's used to treat hypokalemia patients, then warned me to stay the hell away from it because it could kill me."

"Did my sister know that she was dating a drug addict?"

"I am not a drug addict, ma'am. I'm simply a man with needs."

"If you didn't steal the potassium chloride from Ella, how'd you get it?"

Noel bowed his head and batted his eyelashes. "Through the dark web, of course, where you can get virtually anything. Mi loco amigo had that KCl coming in *hot*!"

There it was. That phrase he'd texted to Charlotte. It resonated like sharp nails, penetrating her skin. How ironic that Hunter's use of the phrase had almost incriminated him.

"The dark web, huh," she said. "Duly noted. We'll be sure to inform our digital forensic investigator of that when we turn over your electronics. See if we can hunt down the owner of the site and hit him with charges as well."

Miles nodded. "Copy that."

"C-c-can we get back to that heart I carved into Corporal Kincaid's chest?" Noel sputtered at the detective. "That was a nice little personal touch, wasn't it? An ode to the entire Love family, if you will. I just love, no pun intended, how I combined the whole California serial killer thing with my own personal vendetta against you two."

Miles's stolid expression crumbled into an angry scowl. The moment he opened his mouth to speak, Charlotte grabbed his arm.

"Just tune him out," she said. "His words mean nothing, and he's going to prison for life. This whole ordeal is over."

"You're right. Finally…"

Epilogue

Two months later...

"Are you enjoying being here in Clemmington?" Miles asked Charlotte.

"I am. I'm loving it, actually. This is a nice change of pace from River Valley. And after all that I've been through—rather, *we've* been through—I needed a change of scenery."

"I agree."

Miles sat back in his lawn chair and glanced around his parents' backyard. The colorful philodendron plants and butterfly bushes surrounding the lush green lawn had blossomed since the last time he was there. So had the western redbud tree that stood in the middle of the yard, its magenta-colored blooms blowing gently in the breeze.

The entire Love family and a few close friends were there to celebrate Miles's return and welcome Charlotte, who'd taken a leave from the force. His heart was full, being back home with her by his side.

He kissed the back of her hand, then stood. "May I have everyone's attention, please? First, I'd like to thank all of you for being here today. I don't know how my mother managed to pull this little welcome home gathering off on such short notice, but nevertheless, I appreciate it."

"Anything for my son!" Betty called out.

"While my stint in River Valley was a success, and Charlotte and I managed to capture the Numeric Serial Killer, it feels damn good to be home."

His sister, Lena, raised her glass. "Us having you back in one piece feels even better!"

"Thanks, sis." He turned to Charlotte. "And to you. The woman I fell in love with some time ago and never stopped loving. It may seem odd that we reconnected over a murder investigation, but however it came about, I'm just glad that we did. Words could never convey how excited I am for our future together. You, me and baby Zoe. Thank you for reaching out on that fateful day and asking for my help. More importantly, thank you for not sending me on my way once the case was solved."

"Well, by that time," Charlotte said, pointing at her slightly protruding belly, "I was kind of stuck with you." She paused when the group broke out into laughter. "Seriously, though, you deserve all of my thanks. Not only for assisting me with the biggest investigation of my career, but for showing me that true love hadn't passed me by. I just had to open myself up to it. For that, I will be forever grateful."

"Aww," the crowd sighed as the pair shared a kiss.

"I love you," Miles whispered in her ear.

"I love you, too."

Miles's father, Kennedy, who served as Clemmington's chief of police, waved his hand in the air. "Thank you for those wonderful words, you two. Now that we've toasted to the happy couple, I have some news that I'd like to share. If I may…"

"Of course," Miles said. "You've got the floor."

Betty wrapped her arm around Kennedy, her eyes filling with tears.

"Um," Kennedy began, his voice wavering. "After working for the Clemmington Police Department for almost forty years, I've decided to…to turn in my badge—"

"Wait, *what*!" Jake yelled over the group's stunned gasps. "Dad, you're retiring? When did you decide this?"

"Your mother and I have been discussing it for a while now. It's time, son. I'm no spring chicken. Plus, your mother and I are ready to relax. Get out there and do some traveling. Enjoy life without the stress of an investigation hanging over my head." He pointed toward Miles and Charlotte. "Not to mention we've got our first grandbaby on the way. I'd like to focus on being a grandfather."

The family gathered around and embraced Kennedy. A few tears trickled down his cheeks. Betty patted them away.

"I'm so proud of you, honey," she told him.

Jake pulled away abruptly. "Hold on. Who's gonna take over as Clemmington's new chief?"

"Good question," Miles chimed in.

"As long as it's not my archenemy," Lena interjected, "better known as Detective Russ Campbell, then I'm good with whoever you choose."

Kennedy grabbed a bottle of champagne. "The person I've chosen to run the department," he began, refilling Jake's glass, "is you."

"Me?" Jake whispered.

"Yes. *You.* I've already confirmed it with the mayor."

"Congratulations, baby," Betty told him.

The crowd went wild as champagne splashed everywhere. Miles, Lena and Jake threw their arms around one another and hopped around in a circle. It was a gesture they'd been making since they were children.

Charlotte snapped a photo of the celebration. "Congratulations on your retirement, Chief Love. I can only imagine what life was like in your household back when these three were younger."

"Oh, there was never a dull moment, I can tell you that much."

"Charlotte!" Ella called out as she came running through the back gate. "I am so sorry I'm late."

"Hey," Jake whispered, tugging Miles's arm. "Who is that?"

"You don't recognize her from the video chat? That's Ella. Charlotte's sister."

Jake's mouth fell open as he eyed her. "Oh, yeah. It's all coming back to me now. She's even prettier in person. Is she single?"

"I don't know. Why don't you go and ask her yourself?"

"Smart-ass…" Jake muttered.

Charlotte barely introduced the pair before Jake handed Ella a drink and offered to introduce her to everyone.

"Your brother is a smooth one, isn't he?" she asked Miles.

"Not usually. But there's something about Ella that brings out the Denzel in him."

"Well, while they get to know one another, I think the baby and I are ready for a second helping of barbecue."

"Follow me," Miles said, holding out his arm and leading Charlotte into the kitchen. "I could use a few more ribs and a little quiet time myself. I adore my family, but they can be a bit exhausting to say the least. Are you sure you're gonna be able to handle all the madness that the Love family brings to the table?"

"Absolutely. In fact, nothing would make me happier."

He stood at the counter and stared at her, overcome by a tingling sense of elation.

"Why are you looking at me like that?" Charlotte asked.

"Because I can't believe that this is actually my life. You've gotta understand, I never thought we'd get a second chance. Yet here we are. Together in Clemmington. After solving the case of a lifetime. *And* we're having a baby. I'm just so…so overwhelmed."

"With happiness?" she asked, running her hands along his biceps.

He responded by grabbing hold of her hips, their bodies swaying to the jazz music streaming from the deck. "Of course. And love. And joy. Because I get to spend the rest of my life with the only woman I've ever loved."

"Ditto," Charlotte said as her lips melted into his.

* * * * *

COMING NEXT MONTH FROM

⟨H⟩ HARLEQUIN
INTRIGUE

#2151 TARGETED IN SILVER CREEK
Silver Creek Lawmen: Second Generation • by Delores Fossen

A horrific shooting left pregnant artist Hanna Kendrick with no memory of Deputy Jesse Ryland...nor the night their newborn son was conceived. But when the gunman escapes prison and places Hannah back in his crosshairs, only Jesse can keep his child and the woman he loves safe.

#2152 DISAPPEARANCE IN DREAD HOLLOW
Lookout Mountain Mysteries • by Debra Webb

A crime spree has rocked Sheriff Tara Norwood's quiet town. Her only lead is a missing couple's young son...and the teacher he trusts. Deke Shepherd vows to aid his ex's investigation and protect the boy. But when life-threatening danger and unresolved romance collide, will the stakes be too high?

#2153 CONARD COUNTY: CODE ADAM
Conard County: The Next Generation • by Rachel Lee

Big city detective Valerie Brighton will risk everything to locate her kidnapped niece. Even partner with lawman Guy Redwing, despite reservations about his small-town detective skills. But with bullets flying and time running out, Guy proves he's the only man capable of saving a child's life...and Valerie's jaded heart.

#2154 THE EVIDENCE NEXT DOOR
Kansas City Crime Lab • by Julie Miller

Wounded warrior Grayson Malone has become the KCPD's most brilliant criminologist. When his neighbor Allie Tate is targeted by a stalker, he doesn't hesitate to help. But soon the threats take a terrorizing, psychological toll. And Grayson must provide answers *and* protection to keep her alive.

#2155 OZARKS WITNESS PROTECTION
Arkansas Special Agents • by Maggie Wells

Targeted by her husband's killer, pregnant widow and heiress Kayla Powers needs a protection plan—pronto. But 24/7 bodyguard duty challenges Special Agent Ryan Hastings's security skills...and professional boundaries. Then Kayla volunteers herself as bait to bring the elusive assassin to justice...

#2156 HUNTING A HOMETOWN KILLER
Shield of Honor • by Shelly Bell

FBI Special Agent Rhys Keller has tracked a serial killer to his small mountain hometown—and Julia Harcourt's front door. Safeguarding his world-renowned ex in close quarters resurrects long buried emotions. But will their unexpected reunion end in the murderer's demise...or theirs?

YOU CAN FIND MORE INFORMATION ON UPCOMING HARLEQUIN TITLES, FREE EXCERPTS AND MORE AT HARLEQUIN.COM.

HICNM0523

HARLEQUIN
PLUS

Try the best multimedia subscription service for romance readers like you!

Read, Watch and Play.

Experience the easiest way to get the romance content you crave.

Start your **FREE TRIAL** at
<u>www.harlequinplus.com/freetrial</u>.